16-PSYCHE MINING EXPEDITION

ERIC WILKINS

ISBN:
978-1-952874-78-9 (paperback)
978-1-952874-79-6 (hardback)
978-1-952874-80-2 (ebook)

Published by:

 OMNIBOOK Co.

OMNIBOOK CO.
99 Wall Street, Suite 118
New York, NY 10005
USA
+1-866-216-9965
www.omnibookcompany.com

For e-book purchase: Kindle on Amazon, Barnes and Noble
Book purchase: Amazon.com, Barnes & Noble, and
www.omnibookcompany.com

Omnibook titles may be purchased in bulk for educational,
business, fund-raising, or sales promotional use. For more
information please e-mail info@omnibookcompany.com

CONTENTS

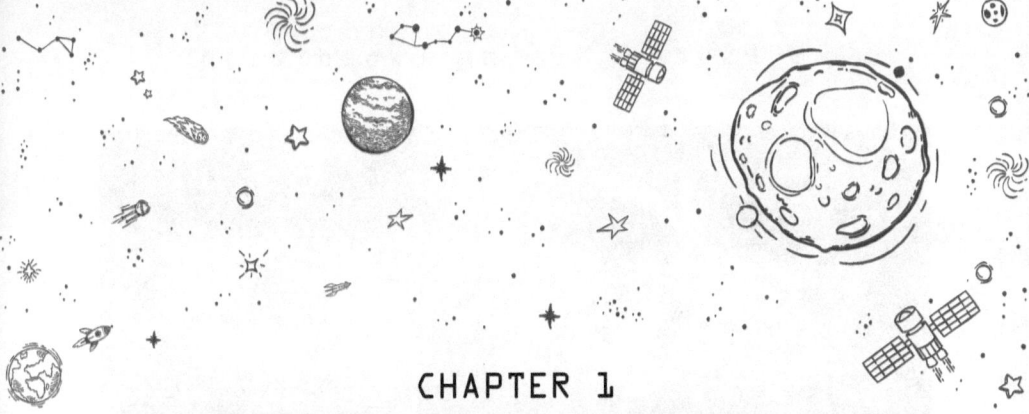

CHAPTER 1
16-PSYCHE MINE-X EXPEDITION

Captain Jonathan Adams's - Updated Report to US Congress and US Space Command at Mine-X Corporation on the status of the 16-Psyche mission that I, head Commander Captain Jonathan Adams, do hereby submit to the proper authorities of the past status of the 16-Psyche mission.

The $900-Quintillion valuable treasure of 16-Psyche was the ultimate end goal of the mission sponsored by Mine-X Corporation. The mission was to land and begin mining the valuable resources of 16-Psyche in the asteroid belt.

This extremely hard-to-accomplish mission was extensively planned over and over the past decade. Three mining vessels had been constructed at the Gateway Moon base station located at the Lagrange point between the Earth and the Moon.

For over a decade, Mine-X Mining Corporation had invested huge assets and resources towards this future adventure to establish a mining base on the surface of 16-Psyche.

16-Psyche exists in the asteroid belt approximately 2.5 AU's from our star, the Sun. 1 AU is equal to approximately 93 million miles or 150 million kilometers. 16-Psyche revolves around the Sun approximately once every five Earth years inside the asteroid belt between the orbits of Mars and Jupiter.

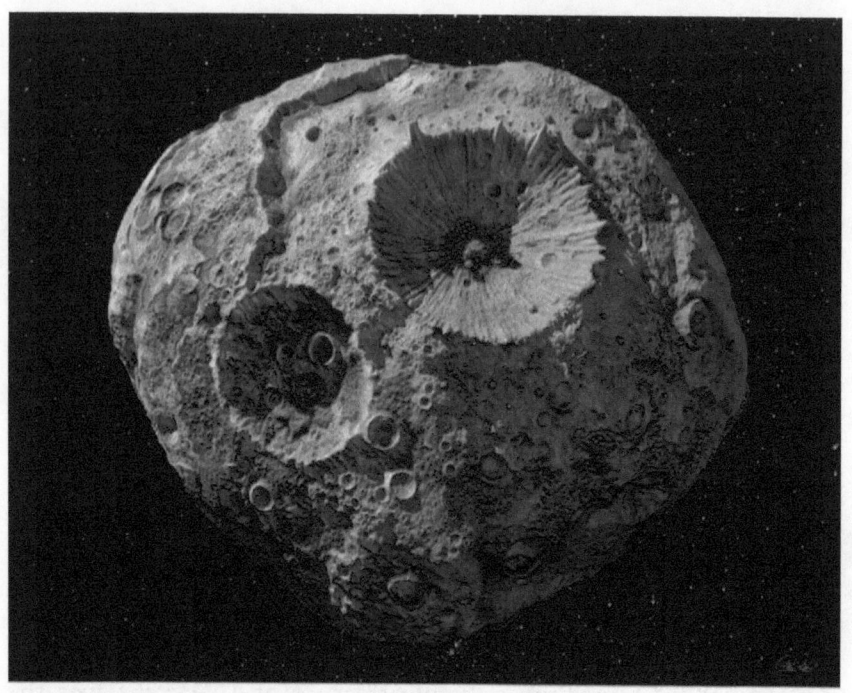

16 Psyche

Beginning in the year 2238, Mine-X Corporation, an ambitious space-mining outfit, had nearly finished constructing three ships at the L1 Gateway Lagrange Point Base. The entire three-ship crew was staffed with a total of a fifty-member team to be launched towards Mars with the first goal of landing all three ships on Phobos, which is the closest Moon of Mars.

The long journey to Phobos would take just over seven months to arrive once the ships departed from the gateway station positioned approximately 45,000 miles above Earth's Moon.

The intention was to land the three mining vessels on Phobos first. Alpha-2 and 3 would set up on Phobos first and test the mining equipment for several months. Once accomplished, The mission would re-supply the three ship's fuel and necessities from Mars base and set out on the journey to begin mining operations on 16-Psyche.

CHAPTER 2

HISTORY'S FIRST LANDING ON MARS

Two hundred and one years ago, the first landing on Planet Mars was accomplished on July 6th of the year 2037.

In those long ago early days, an expedition of seven astronauts first landed upon Phobos in preparation for four of the astronauts to attempt a safe first landing on Planet Mars.

The very first soft landing on Phobos on a ship named *Challenger-2* was accomplished on June 21st in the year 2037. Two weeks after first landing on Phobos, the seven had partially explored the immediate area of Phobos while studying the surface of the beautiful Mars world below.

Phobos was easier to land Challenger-2 on in those early space exploration times than Mars because of its gentle easy gravity. One side of Phobos always faces towards the majestic Mars world below.

A suited astronaut on the surface of Phobos would only weigh approximately two to four ounces.

The entire early Mars landing craft and crew had a huge mass and weighed many tons in earth gravity, but the Challenger-2 vessel only weighed approximately two hundred pounds once it gently touched down on Phobos for the first time.

The Mars landing took place 68 years after Neil Armstrong and Buzz Aldrin first stepped upon Earth's Moon.

Humans of my generation now had new heroes to honor.

On July 20th, 2037, Charlotte Elliott, Alexia Justice, Eric Stencil, and Robert Pesto were the first humans to descend from Phobos and step upon the surface of Planet Mars.

Charlotte Elliott's footprints were the first human steps to be placed on Mars on that long ago day.

Three other astronauts named Joshua Tibens, Scarlet Meshing, and Yasmin Topaz remained on Phobos and monitored the first human descent to the surface. Several 24-hour periods later, the three joined the four that had first landed and set up a temporary base.

I, Jonathan Adams, two centuries later, at 21, had recently graduated from the Space Launch Academy Headquarters in Titusville, Florida. I was newly assigned to lead the mining expedition to the supposed metal core asteroid called *16-Psyche* in the asteroid belt.

In the year 2022, it is recorded that a robotic satellite was launched to the 16-Psyche asteroid to gain more knowledge about this has been 500-mile diameter world that existed long ago before having its surface blown away during a cataclysmic collision.

CHAPTER 3

ANNIBALE DE GASPARIS' DISCOVERY

The asteroid 16-Psyche was first discovered by telescope by Annibale de Gasparis, an Italian astronomer from Naples, in 1852.

Psyche received its name after a Greek mythological figure from the myth of Cupid. Psyche was perceived to be a beautiful mortal girl who had a romance with Venus. Venus became jealous and angry, and she put Psyche through many hardships and trials. In conclusion, Cupid asked Jupiter to make Psyche immortal and present it to him in marriage, which Jupiter does.

The "16" prefix is added because it was the sixteenth of the minor planets to be discovered in chronological order.

Depending on the moment, Psyche is between 1.5 and 2.3 Astronomical Units from Earth. That's anywhere from 139 million to 214 million miles. The reason why the distance is not constant is that the orbits of both Earth and 16-Psyche are elliptical, so there are points in their orbits when they are farther away, and at other times, they are closer together.

Years ago, the first robotic satellite mission to 16-Psyche was launched from Earth at an optimal launch point on August 18th, 2022.

In the present year of 2238, Mine-X Corporation hired me to head the first mining attempt in the asteroid belt.

My assignment was to head up the mining journey to the highly dense metal-estimated 900 Quintillion dollar valued core of 16-Psyche that orbits the Sun once every five earth years in the asteroid belt.

CHAPTER 4

PHOBOS KNOWN FACTS

Phobos is the potato-shaped Mars Moon, approximately 17x14x11 miles or 27x22x18 kilometers in diameter. Phobos's total orbital distance of roughly 5,826 miles (9,376 km) from Mars. The Moon revolves around Mars in a speedy easterly direction.

In other words, Phobos moves almost twice as fast as the planet Mars and rotates along its orbital path as Mars goes around the Sun. Every hundred years, Phobos is spiraling closer to Mars. The difference in the distance every century is equal to around 6 feet 7 inches or 2 meters.

That equals to less than 80% of an inch per earth-year. This close distance between Phobos and Mars is the closest that has ever been discovered in the entire solar system. Phobos has an orbital period equal to one Mars orbit every 7.7 earth hours. Phobos orbits eastward faster than Mars rotates.

It is surmised that if the orbit of Phobos is uninterrupted and left unchanged for 50 million years or so, Phobos will eventually break up and crash into Mars, or it may disintegrate when it reaches the gravity Roche limit and allow Mars to one day have a ring system.

Phobos orbits Mars in the same direction that Mars rotates, but it is moving so fast that it races around the planet every 7.7 hours or almost three times in one 24-hour and 37-minute Mars day.

A large part of both Mars moons are indeed carbon-rich rock, but that isn't all. Scientists perceived that Phobos and Deimos are made of carbon rock and frozen water ice. More recent studies into Phobos indicate that the outer surface is covered with a layer of dust regolith approximately one meter thick.

An astronaut who weighs 68 kilograms or 150 pounds on Earth would weigh about 40 gram-force or 2 ounces standing on the surface of Phobos. So, an astronaut would weigh less than 4 ounces in a space suit.

Indeed, attempting to walk as light as a feather on the one-meter-thick regolith surface of Phobos would be like walking on a snowy frozen sponge. A new version of astronaut shoe spikes would soon become necessary in any surface-walking attempt on the Mars Moon named Phobos.

Three exploration-mining vessels were now finished being constructed, and I, Captain Jonathan Adams, was assigned to the largest of the three vessels stationed just outside Gateway Base-L1. (Lagrange 1)

CHAPTER 5
ALPHA-1'S DETAILS

My lead ship, named *Alpha-1*, was the main command center for the three-ship venture soon to be launched towards the Mars moon Phobos. Alpha-1's size, color, and shape would appear like a silver eight-sided double-stacked half-kilometer in diameter stop sign with the main engines concealed beneath one of its eight sides.

Alpha-2 and *Alpha-3* were white 750 feet diameter half-ball-shaped mining vessels that were half the size of Alpha-1 but still appeared formidable in size as I approached my new command station aboard Alpha-1 in a shuttlecraft.

I first boarded Alpha-1 twenty-four hours before the journey to Phobos would depart from the vicinity of Gateway base near Earth's Moon.

Captain Candice Roselle was commanding Alpha-2 with nine crew aboard her mining vessel.

The Alpha-3 mining vessel was assigned to a young captain named Austin Williams and his nine crew, who were willing and ready to begin the first stage of this dangerous mission to 16-Psyche.

Alpha-1 was constructed to be the central command ship and living quarters for its 30-member crew and, if necessary, house all 50 crewmembers.

My mission was for Alpha-1 to be launched from Gateway Base first. Then, Alpha-2 and 3 would be launched each on a two-week separate schedule behind Alpha-1.

It was best decided that this was a wise travel method toward Phobos. If an emergency should occur, a rescue could be accomplished by any of the three ships.

Upon being the first to arrive, it was the Alpha-1 crew's duty to use that separation time to explore and decide the best area on Phobos to land the two mining ships Alpha-2 and 3 when they arrived separately two weeks apart.

Alpha-2 and 3 were nearly identical in appearance. Best described visually, they appeared to be a white half-ball-shaped Pac-Man that is 750 feet in diameter. Jagged drilling teeth on the bottom edge attracted your vision to the glistening steel blades that were intended to rotate and dig once operational on the surface of Phobos and then, later on, to grind into the valuable metal resources of 16-Psyche.

Alpha-2 and 3 vessels were the mining drills themselves. Once landed and operational, the ship's bottom center would be secured on a hydraulic pedestal, and the outside perimeter blades would grind down slowly and harvest the resources in a mining operation.

Once a ship ground down several meters, the outer grinding rings would stop, and the product gained would be introduced into a cargo pod at the ship's central processing facility.

Once a cylinder container was loaded, the cargo pod would be launched on a space glide path back in the direction of Planet Earth.

Upon completing this historic mission, Mine-X Corporation will release its report of the chronicles of this hard-to-accomplish mining venture.

January 6th, 2238- Alpha-1 to Phobos

There is no day and night in space, but hours and 24-hour periods were still used in this description of this great beginning of Alpha-1 leaving for Mars. Earth time was still the base rule for the measurement of time.

It would have been 8 AM EST on Earth this day of 1-6-2238 as I, Jonathan, readied Alpha-1 to begin its hard-to-accomplish journey.

One silver and two white ships that had been built at Gateway base over the past decade were slowly orbiting the station at a distance of 50 kilometers.

Alpha-1 was twice the size of the two white doughnut-shaped mines digging Alpha-2 and 3 vessels. Its eight-sided shape and double-layer crew quarter appearance made it easy to distinguish from the ships to follow in two-week intervals.

Gateway Base is located at the L-1 Lagrange point of approximately 70,000 kilometers or 43,495 miles above Earth's Moon. Super ion propulsion engines that enabled slow propulsion at the start but would increase speed slowly as each minute passed were the power source for all three ships.

Each ship was also equipped with a main nuclear engine that even had the capability of landing on Mars should it become necessary. But landing on Mars was not the purpose of this perilous mission. Phobos would be the destination, and although Phobos had certain valuable minerals, the primary purpose on Phobos was to test the mining equipment before the goal of landing and mining 16-Psyche in order to obtain the valuable pure metals that existed only on that small world.

CHAPTER 6
DEPARTURE FROM GATEWAY

Earth Eastern Standard Time of 0800 hours, I, Captain Adams, gave the order to engage the Ion engines and slowly sail away from the Gateway Base Complex. Alpha-1 gradually sailed away from the Gateway Complex, where all three ships had been assembled over the past decade.

It was a seven-month-long voyage to reach Mars, and Mars was now at the proper place in its orbit to provide a six-week launch window necessary for all three ships to be launched in sequence.

Alpha-1 was now on its way to accomplish the first step in getting to the Mars Moon Phobos. Alpha-2 would be launched in two weeks' earth time and Alpha-3 two weeks after Alpha-2.

On board on 1st ship were myself and 29 space miners that would be the crew that would land on Phobos, ahead of the other two ships, to set up the first steps of testing the two mining ships once their landing site had been chosen.

These events couldn't occur until the seven-month travel time it would require for Alpha-1 and crew to arrive in the vicinity of Mars and the intended Moon destination of Phobos.

The crew watched as the visibility of Gateway Base slowly became a bright point hanging slightly above Earth's Moon, defining the entire view of the smaller Earth-Moon system.

Alpha 1's first objective was to achieve Earth's gravity well escape velocity of approximately eight miles per second relative to the Earth.

That equates to just over 28,800 miles per hour or 46,349 kph. But one must realize this important fact. Speed in space is relative to what object you are referring the speed to. No object in space is standing still. Everything is always moving. Right now, Alpha-1 was traveling at a rate of 8 mps away from Gateway base and the Earth-Moon gravity well system.

Alpha-1 measured almost 1500 feet in diameter across, and its 15-meter tall two-story decking capacity vibrated a bit as the main engines were engaged in achieving escape velocity of the Earth-Moon gravity well system. Once completed, the intention was to shut the engines down and coast for seven months to a Mars interception.

There is indeed a logical reason for this long coasting voyage. There's an unforgivable space certainty fact that states, for any amount of speed obtained from propulsion, the same amount of energy would have to be used to cancel out that forward velocity once a destination has been achieved. The Mars coasting journey was considered the best possible option for all three ships.

Two hours 38 minutes after Alpha-1 had left Gateway base, the ship had gained the velocity of 8.2 miles per second from the Gateway complex. Alpha-1 was traveling 29,520 miles per hour towards its rendezvous with Mars. That's relative to the Earth-Moon system.

There was now a silence when all engines had ceased. Now, all eight ninety-degree angled ion-powered nozzles propelled Alpha-1 into one revolution every 30-second spin or two revolutions per minute.

Six solar panels began deploying and tracking the Sun. There were three on each side of the ship. With a slow-programmed direction, they began unfolding simultaneously. After a two-minute spring-loaded release, all solar panels locked into place and started a combined focused lock on tracking the Sun as the ship rotated to allow 10% gravity inside the walls of Alpha-1.

From the outside, long lines of cabin lights were all that were visible as Alpha-1 sailed silently through the dark black void of outer space. Its destination, towards where planet Mars would be in its orbit seven months from Alpha-1's launch.

Alpha-1 appeared as a rotating silver octagon-shaped ship with six gold solar panels, three on each side, rotating and tracking our star, the Sun. The ship had achieved all the speed required in order to achieve its Mars-bound goal.

My First officer Melissa Harper had been in command of the entire launch sequence, and now that Alpha-1 was rotating, the outer deck quarters were experiencing approximately 20% Earth-gravity with the floors pointing towards the outward spin of Alpha-1's rotation.

The ten-meter diameter clear dome command deck sat above and forward of one of the eight sides on top of Alpha-1. The command deck shifted its angle 90% due to the gravity that the rotation of Alpha-1 was causing. We were now looking up and back towards the rear of three solar panels on each side located above and below us. We watched the panels rotate once every 30 seconds while tracking the Sun.

Melissa engaged the ship's autopilot, and as the fifth hour from departure had passed, Alpha-1 and Crew were now on their Mars-bound glide path towards unknown future adventures.

All crew stations had reported in, and twenty-eight crewmembers scattered to different sections of the ship to begin performing their experiments and duties. In twenty-four hours, the ship had traveled over 708,480 miles, and in two weeks, when Alpha-2 will be launched, there will be a separation distance between Alpha-1 and 2 of nearly 9,918,720 miles or 15,962,632 kilometers. By the time Alpha-1 reaches Mars, the ship will have traveled approximately 148,780,800 miles or 239,439,488 kilometers.

Mars is approximately 50 million miles from Earth when the two worlds are closest to each other or in conjunction, but Alpha 1's glide path had to travel a long curved arc nearly three times the distance from Earth to Mars. Each ship had to be launched towards a point where Mars would be in its orbit seven months from each ship's launch date.

Alpha-1 had sailed without incident for two weeks when Gateway Base had verified that Alpha-2 had been launched and was now nearly ten million miles behind us and was traveling at a relative speed to our ship.

A 54-second communication delay each way between Alpha-1 and 2 was not a real issue. The communication time delay would remain all the way to Mars and double to approximately two minutes between Alpha-1 and 3.

Commander Austin Williams would command Alpha-3 and bring up the three-ship convoy's rear to the Mars Moon called *Phobos*.

Alpha-1 sailed silently onward for two more weeks when the confirmation of Alpha-3's launch was confirmed. Communication was now enabled between the entire convoy, and the distance and time it took for light wave transmissions would vary as each vessel was spaced 10 million miles between each other. Everything had progressed normally into the tenth week or a third of our journeys towards Mars rendezvous. That was until Day-77 of the mission.

CHAPTER 7
ALPHA-1 STRUCK BY METEOR

A meteor suddenly struck the ship near the center cargo storage area. Alpha 1 was spewing gasses into space from the still rotating spin of the ship.

Melissa and I were shocked by the cataclysmic event that had just occurred without any warning. Alarms sounded, and lights flashed as She and I struggled to get back into the ship's command control stations and strap ourselves in.

I scanned the ship's computers to discern significant damage control. At the same time, Melissa began engaging secondary backup power and started the process of attempting to bring Alpha-1 out of its now wobbly rotation. Slowly but surely, Melissa was able to get Alpha-1 under control. Damage control reports were being calculating, and programmed corrections were being input into the computer.

The computer is reporting that there's a foot diameter hole in the center cargo area. Several oxygen-welding tanks were damaged, and the remainder of that gas is still leaking into space.

Two crew were in that department before they were sealed off and presumed to be deceased. An unknown object crashed into the ship and exploded two welding cylinders in storage compartment six.

That compartment storage area has now been sealed off, and actions are underway for suited-up astronauts to retrieve the two bodies in the decompressed cargo bay.

The ship's status is not severe, but one of the six solar panels has been disabled due to the crash incident. An outside EVA will have to be performed to determine the extent of panel damage while also repairing the hole above compartment 6 storage chamber.

The computer's feminine voice finished its initial damage report as Melissa, and I realized the seriousness of the situation. Two of the crew had been inside cargo bay six when the impact occurred and exploded the welding cylinders. Now sealed off from the ship, two male frozen bodies floated inside the airless bay with a one-foot jagged hole in its ceiling.

Alpha-1 appeared idle as if it were drifting, but in reality, the ship was still moving along at eight miles per second towards Mars. There was no gravity aboard for several days while outside EVA repair sorties were being performed to weld and repair damage to the cargo bay and the damaged solar array.

Day-91 since departure and two weeks after the collision incident, Alpha-1 was fully repaired. The ship is now back in rotation and nearly halfway to Mars. For two weeks, the crew had been so involved in repairing the ship that they hadn't had time yet to have a memorial service for the two astronauts lost in the collision.

CHAPTER 8
CEREMONY FOR TWO HEROES

Day-101

The entire remaining crew of 28 gathered to honor their two lost friends. As Head Commander Jonathan Adams, I officiated the service to honor Mission Specialist Scott Warden and Specialist Brandon Thistle.

I began my officiating ceremony with these words. "We all knew the risk, and it indeed still exists ahead. On Day-77, these two heroes served with the highest honor. At that time, these heroes made the ultimate sacrifice. They gave their Lives."

We now submit their bodies into the vacuum of space and ask that the Universal Creator will forever guide their way to their next mission.

Moments of silence occurred as their bodies were silently ejected into the cold void of space. We all knew that it could have happened to any of us. We were all grateful that the ship's damage wasn't too bad. Now that repairs had been accomplished, we all respectfully adjourned the service.

We all defiantly knew that the first part of the mission to reach Phobos was still the main objective. In the days ahead, as we dealt with the loss of two of our friends, we became even more focused on our duties to keep Alpha-1 operational and in top shape for landing upon arrival.

Alpha-1 sailed on without further incident. After another four weeks, on Day-142, we could view Mars on the long-range viewer, and the planet was almost the size of a golf ball held at arm's length.

Extreme magnification revealed the moon Phobos as it traveled its circle orbit east to west around Mars. Under Magnification, Phobos appeared only as a small potato-shaped shadow as it eclipsed a sliver of Mar's rusty tinted surface hue.

CHAPTER 9

DAY-180 THROUGH DAY-210 ABOARD ALPHA-1

On this day, a crew of eight ship specialists gathered among the gallery to discuss the present mission status and the status of Alpha-1. I, Jonathan Adams, started the scheduled meeting requesting the attention of the convened eight before me.

I then instructed my first officer Melissa to begin reporting the ship's overall present status.

There are a few minor ship problems. There are still some outside ammonia lines that need repairing, but those line issues can easily be repaired once we land on Phobos. Presently the line issues do not affect any of Alpha's systems. Alpha-1 is in good shape, and the ship's total status is rated at 98 percent. Melissa then slowly sat down in the light gravity after finishing her short report.

I stood up and began my words. We all miss out on two lost friends. But I am here to tell you that I'm proud of each and every member aboard.

Alpha-1 is a half-kilometer diameter vessel. This ship has a huge mass and is traveling along at eight miles distance for every second that passes. Right now, Alpha-1 is a month away from Mars orbit insertion. These next thirty days are the most important yet. It will require extreme focus and teamwork to bring this ship's speed down to a perfect orbit insertion speed.

When Mars is viewed from above the North Pole, Mars rotates eastward or in a counter-clockwise direction once in just over twenty-four hours and 37 minutes.

Mars, compared to Earth in size, is estimated to be only 4220 miles or 6791 kilometers in diameter, whereas Earth is over 12,756 kilometers or 7926 miles in diameter. Phobos in its orbit travels only 3,700 miles or 6,000 kilometers above the Martian surface.

Phobos zooms around the red planet almost three times a Martian day. The moon crosses the sky in about four hours. The moon appears from the surface to rise in the west and set in the east.

This crew as a team will have to work together vicariously to begin preparation in the next thirty days to approach the moon and land properly. We have a great crew, and I know we can accomplish our mission without any further loss of life. I have faith in this crew and this ship.

We will soon accomplish the first stage of our mission. Once landed and a base is set up, when Alpha-2 and 3 arrive, we will be exploring the surface and begin testing the mining ships before leaving Phobos to journey onward towards our ultimate goal of landing on and mining 16-Psyche.

With that said, I hereby conclude my status report with the good news that all is on schedule with Alpha-2 and 3, and each ship has reported no major issues thus far. In final conclusion, I hereby submit to all involved this fact sheet of known facts about Phobos.

CHAPTER 10

MORE ABOUT PHOBOS

Phobos is the larger of the two Mars moons and is 17 x 14 x 11 miles or 27 by 22 by 18 kilometers in diameter. The small moon orbits Mars three times a day so close to the planet's surface that it cannot always be seen in some locations on Mars.

Phobos is getting closer to Mars by six feet or 1.8 meters every hundred years. It is predicted that at that rate, it will either crash into Mars in 50 million years or break up into a rocky ringed orbital belt.

The most prominent feature on Phobos is the 6-mile or 9.7-kilometer crater named *Stickney Crater.* Whatever struck the moon caused streak patterns across the surface. Stickney Crater was surpassingly filled with fine dust with some evidence of boulders sliding down its sloped surface.

A labeled crater map was included at the end of the Phobos report. This map would allow us on Alpha-1 to decide on the best possible landing sites for all three ships.

On Day-200 of our voyage, we were only ten days away from Mars orbit insertion. Planet Mars appeared on our view screen as large as a baseball, and the two moons were easily tracked on our forward scanners.

In those final ten days, Alpha-1 and crew were doing their research to make sure no mistakes in calculations were being made. Each crew member was totally focused on their duties and preparation for the landing attempt on Phobos.

Minor adjustments were made to put Alpha-1 on the precise course needed to accomplish the upcoming goal of first entering the orbit of Mars from west to east direction in order to chase and rendezvous with the tiny moon Phobos.

CHAPTER 11

24 HOURS TO MARS INSERTION ORBIT

Our crew of 27 and myself gathered among the conference quarters at 8:30 AM that morning to discuss the final details of the approaching Planet Mars. Calculations for the insertion burn of Alpha's engines were confirmed, and many other steps were agreed upon that would follow as soon as Mars orbit was achieved.

Once achieved, Alpha-1 would have to approach Phobos cautiously, perform an extremely delicate maneuver to match the moon's orbital speed, and attempt to gradually close in and orbit Phobos for a few hours before a finale-landing site would be chosen.

Step two, Once Alpha has successfully landed on Phobos, we must first engage all four-leg screw anchors into the dusty layer matter to ensure that Alpha is secured to the surface.

Phobos has a very light gravity, and the entire weight of this enormous mass ship would weigh less than a few hundred-earth pounds on Phobos. Ultimately, any suited astronaut on the surface would weigh no more than four ounces. Special surface boots would be provided when Phobos EVA's would be performed.

Phobos escape speed was only approximately 25 miles per hour. If it was attempted, and of course, it would not be, a surface astronaut could possibly jump off the moon. If not entirely away from the moon, an astronaut with practice could push off and sail long silent glides over the surface of Phobos.

Years ago, Phobos was used before the first landing on Mars, but Phobos in those days by astronauts was never really explored very much. That certainly would be a priority task for our crew once established upon the surface.

The first main exploration expedition goal would be to explore the mysterious monolith that had been photographed by earlier satellites. We were now attempting to choose the best landing site that was accordingly near the area of this monolith mystery.

The Phobos monolith is a large pillar located on the surface of Mars's moon Phobos. It measured about 279 ft across and 300 feet in height. The monolith on Phobos is a dark object near the Stickney crater. It's approximately the size of a building and casts a prominent shadow on the surface.

A NASA scientist named Efrain Palermo first discovered the monolith on Phobos long ago. That fact was later confirmed by Lan Fleming, an imaging sub-contractor at NASA Johnson Space Center many years ago.

A monolith is a geological feature consisting of a single massive piece of rock. Monoliths do occur naturally on Earth. Never before had the site near Stickney Crater been explored. When we have successfully landed and secured the ship to the surface, the monolith mission would be our first expedition sortie on the surface.

Alpha's engines came to life as Melissa and I monitored the course the ship was experiencing as it fell above the eastern hemisphere of Planet Mars. Alpha was traveling 24.1 kilometers or 14.97 miles per second as it fell towards the speed that Mars was traveling in orbit around the Sun. Phobos orbited Mars at a rate of 2.18 kilometers or 1.32 miles per second in relation to the Mars surface.

Alpha-1 was now falling inward approximately a thousand miles behind Phobos in its eastward orbit, just 6,000 kilometers above the Martian surface and slowly approaching Phobos' 1.32 miles per second orbital speed of Mars. Phobos and Alpha would orbit Mars three revolutions before Alpha-1 would slowly match the moon's speed and approach the exact point of Phobos orbit insertion.

The precarious task of the 150-ton heavy earth mass of Alpha's orbit insertion of the light gravity of Phobos would have to be accomplished before landing. In order for the ship's mass to land gently on Phobos, the entire ship would weigh less than a few hundred-earth pounds in the gravity of Phobos.

CHAPTER 12

LANDING ON PHOBOS

The next 21 hours passed as Alpha-1 was within two hours of maneuvering a precise orbital track around Phobos. When the time arrived, Alpha's engines engaged to perform the precise required vector to pass in front of the Moon's direction and slow to almost 1.2 miles per second in relation to Phobos to achieve orbit.

The ship's first orbit was nearly 2 miles by an oblong 6 miles behind the Moon's travel direction. Suttle changes were made in the first orbit to round off the orbit to a circular two miles above the surface of Phobos.

It was a serene and amazing view speeding above Mars and viewing the rolling rusty-colored mountain landmass below while the ship circled a two-mile high orbit of Phobos. Phobos is tidally locked to Mars, as the Earth's Moon is to Earth.

Alpha-1 now descended past the 5,000 feet level and was headed directly towards a certain chosen surface to the left and above the infamous Stickney Crater.

Sporadic reverse downward engine pulses were emitted from Alpha-1 as it eased ever so slowly downward until it touched the surface as light as a feather. After settling from a slight bounce, the ship instantly engaged its screw legs a half-meter deep into Phobos's soft regolith. Dust floated like snowflakes around the ship for an hour after Alpha-1 had landed.

The entire crew of 28 let out a combined rejoice celebration yell as Alpha-1 had accomplished the first step of eventually completing their intended journey to the extreme riches of 16-Psyche.

The low gravity of Phobos settled through the enclosed structure of Alpha-1. Gravity was so low that it was almost like there was no gravity at all. Four hours after landing, the crew was busy checking out the ship's status, and the first EVA would be performed on Day-214 once the selected three astronauts had received eight hours of sleep before the Monolith expedition could begin.

Day-212 from launch, Alpha-1 had softly touched down and secured itself in a somewhat flat area between *Roche* and *Gulliver Crater*. Alpha and crew were now safe. Several hours of station keeping occurred before an expedition of three astronauts was chosen to explore the immediate area around the ship.

Ship specialists Shanta Jackson, Bristol Dole, and Fredrick Crews were the three astronauts that now suited up in the decompression chamber. Red, green, and gold stripes on the sleeves of their white space suits. To distinguish their identity: Shanta wore red, Bristol wore green, and Fredrick wore the gold stripes on his suit sleeves.

The team of three wore bubble front clear shields that covered their heads, and the twistable ball bearing helmet attachment allowed the astronauts to have a 270-degree vision while outside on the surface.

Their unique space boots were an amazing invention that was created just for this low gravity situation on the surface of Phobos and 16-Psyche. In appearance, these boots had snowshoe-like bottoms with retractable curved claws around the bottom and above the claws was a four-inch thick platform compression spring-loaded device. Each boot could be loaded and released to launch an astronaut in any lateral direction when activated. The spring device would enable astronauts to accomplish long easy glides above and over the surface of Phobos.

These special boots could only be spring-loaded to launch an astronaut at a maximum of approximately six miles per hour. That was assumed enough to launch a four-ounce suited astronaut over a kilometer or so from their departure location. Much lower spring release settings could also allow short ten-meter strides when needed.

The door to the outside swished open as the chamber finished releasing the remaining airlock pressure. Shanta Jackson, with snowshoe-like spring boots, was the first to go out on the meter-thick dusty surface of Phobos. Her less than four-ounce weight hardly made an indentation in the fine dusty regolith soil.

Bristol Dole and Frederick Crews also ejected from the hatch with their controllable boot claws digging four inches into the regolith beneath their boots when they landed. The three tilted their heads and bodies back and, for the first time, directly viewed the amazing Mars rolling by with the blackness of space surrounding the rusty surface edge.

It was as if the Moon they were riding was a slow rolling eastward display of the same direction-rotating surface below. Phobos was traveling around Mars once every 7.6 hours and was traveling way faster than the 24-hour 37-minute day of Mars. If you were standing on the surface of Mars, Phobos would appear to rise in the west, and after a third of a Mars day, the Moon would set in the east.

Walking on this low gravity surface proved almost impossible and very awkward. Shanta was the first to try out her experimental launch boots. She cautiously began her first test with a ten percent setting that would only launch her no more than ten meters.

She leaned a bit forward in the direction she intended to go and released a ten percent spring-thrust, and surface matter dust ejected from her soles and scattered like snowflakes in the opposite direction that she was traveling. Shanta rose from the surface as gentle as a feather in soft wind and, in ten seconds, slowly settled from a forward 45-degree landing on her snow-shoed boots about thirty feet away from Bristol and Frederick.

As soon as her boots had touched the surface, the four-inch curved spikes engaged, and each boot instantly dug into the regolith, and she was able to stabilize her forward motion. Frederick and Bristol began testing their spring propulsion boots and separately investigated the immediate area surrounding Alpha-1.

Specialist Bristol Dole had already assailed to the top of Alpha-1 with a first duty detail of retracting the 50-meter tall antenna back into position to have better surface contact and communications with the fast approaching Alpha-2 and 3 ships. Alpha-2 was presently just over twelve days away from arrival.

Alpha's screw leg anchors had leveled the ship as much as possible. But, the low gravity didn't change the crewmembers' flight maneuvering ability inside the ship enough to be noticeable. The crew sailed like birds gracefully here and there inside the ship, almost like gravity didn't exist at all.

Fredrick had finished setting up a 360 camera viewing station, and Shanta was finishing setting up seismometer equipment a hundred yards away near the edge of Stickney Crater.

Six hours of the first EVA had passed when Melissa informed the three on the surface that Jonathan Adams had given the order for them to finish up their activities and re-enter the ship as soon as possible.

The astronauts took one more last look around at the beautiful, hard-to-explain fantastic view they were experiencing before all three gracefully glided through the hatch to the airlock chamber.

They had spent 6 hours and 15 minutes on the surface, and all early equipment set-ups had been accomplished. The spring-loaded space boots had been a great asset in the ability to move around on the light gravity Moon. The crew was delighted with the first sortie's success outside the ship.

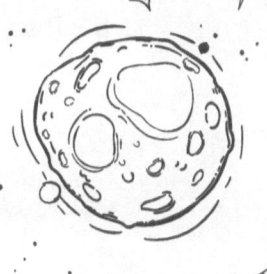

CHAPTER 13

THE MONOLITH ON PHOBOS

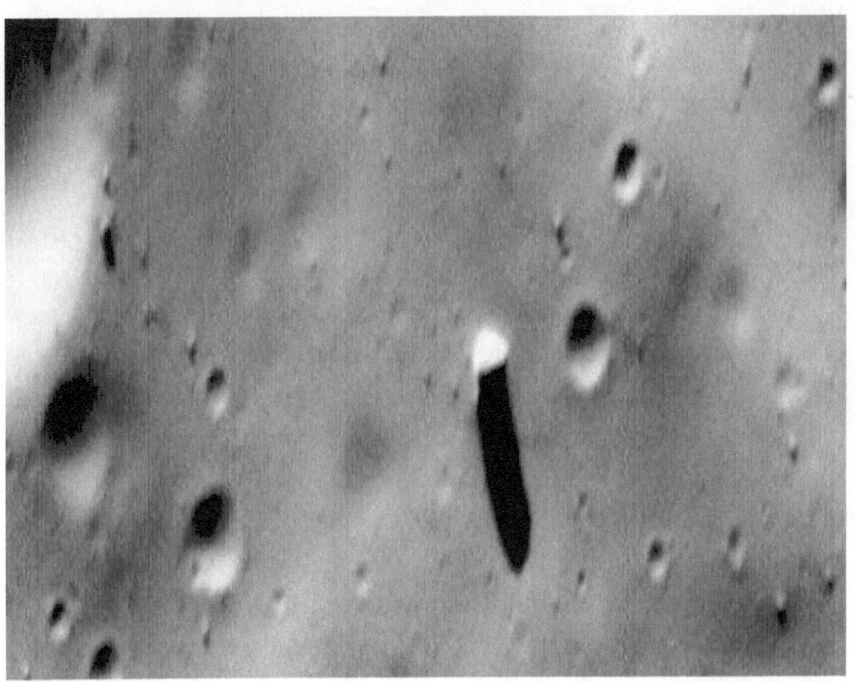

Phobos Monolith

This mysterious *Phobos Monolith* exists a mile or so near the crest of Stickney Crater.

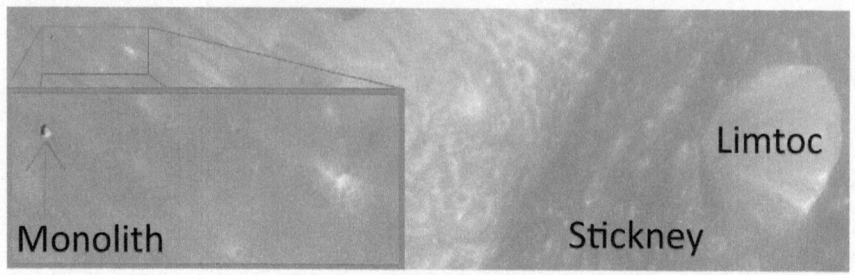

Location of the Monolith

Twenty-four hours later, on Day-215, a team of five, including Melissa and myself, gently floated through the airlock. Our first experience was to travel to the edge of Stickney Crater and gaze into the vast crater that had another large crater inside of the deep giant depression called *Limtoc Crater*.

The giant Stickney Crater was over 9 kilometers or 5.6 miles in diameter. The Limtoc Crater near the top of the massive Stickney Crater had a diameter of 1.2 miles or 1.9 kilometers.

We all paused a few moments at Stickney's edge to take in the view of the giant vast deep double cavern below that had evidently been caused by some huge collision eons ago. Stickney was fascinating, but it was not the objective of this second EVA excursion. Stickney and Limtoc would be sortie number three on Day-216 if all went well with today's Monolith excursion that was the first objective of this mission exploration.

Subsequently, as the ship commander, I instructed the crew that it was time to head away from Stickney's edge and proceed on our intended mission in the direction where the Phobos Monolith existed. The monolith is located several kilometers outside the middle of the western edge of Stickney Crater on Phobos.

Five spring-launched astronauts now engaged 40 percent spring power and sailed in formation. In nearly 60 seconds, the team floated down, landed approximately a kilometer away, and accomplished a third of the distance needed to reach the Monolith location.

As soon as it was determined that they all were safe, we again launched together on another half-kilometer distance towards the awaiting structure of the giant rock. We landed safely as a team.

Phobos was so curved that from this distance of another half-kilometer away, the jagged edge of a tall cliff overhung and obscured our total view so that only the top of the monolith was visible.

Careful calibrations were then made that would enable our space boots to send us sailing over the edge of the giant cliff and land 30-meters away from the base of the monolith. Our spacesuits also had tiny side direction jet controls that could easily enable the exact landing ability required.

Over the jagged overhang, we launched one at a time and sailed in a sequence of 50 seconds intervals. I, Jonathan Adams, was the first to touch down in front of the majestic skyrocketing structure that towered above me and pointed directly towards Mars below.

The other four touched down behind me one at a time as I stood assimilating the immediate area. For minutes we stood there awestruck as we looked ponderously at the tall black obelisk's base that was still 30-meters away.

Even at this distance, the structure's presence filled most of our forward visual range capacity. In ten-second intervals, we exerted a small spring force and Shanta was the first to settle near the base center edge about ten feet away from the bottom of the giant dark-colored obelisk.

As a team, we stood there in extreme awe as Shanta bounced two meters closer and managed to maneuver a few inches closer in order to reach down and brush the dust away from a small section just above the dusty regolith surface edge.

"Look at this!" she excitedly exclaimed out to the others. "There's something strange here. Everyone need to see this for themselves." Four suited astronauts now landed and semi-circled around behind Shanta. It's some sort of picture graph. It looks Egyptian-like, but it is uniquely different in many unique ways.

Shanta finished brushing the dust away and revealed eight weird symbols like none that had ever been seen before.

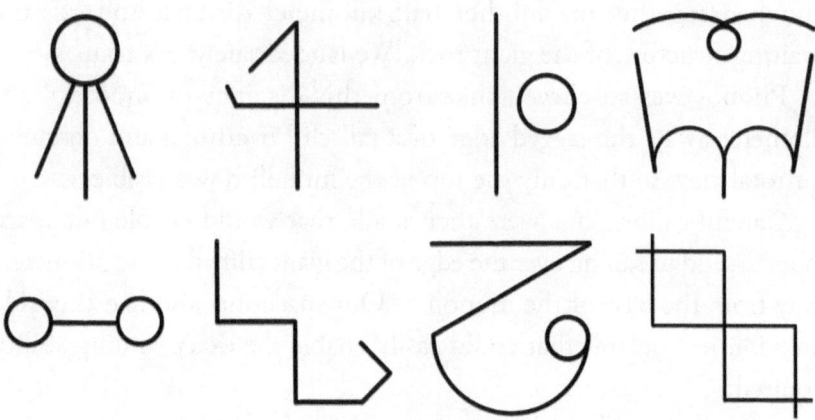

It was amazing. None of us had ever seen any symbols like this before. Each of the eight was embellished in a golden hue and measured about two square inches. The coal-black surface of the giant monolith's side was more than 85 meters or 279 feet wide at the base, and the height rose above 90 meters or approximately 300 feet tall. High above the monolith top, a curled jagged cliff was towering a kilometer above the top of the monolith.

Frederick Crews requested permission to attempt to launch to the top of the monolith. After careful consideration, I gave Crews permission to launch to the top, and four of us watched him soar upward.

Frederick rose up in a slow climb using his suit thruster to guide his way to the very top of the infamous monolith.

Much to his surprise, when he landed, the very flat top of the monolith was covered with two inches of dust and trapezoid-shaped on top. He gently settled on top, and his boots instantly dug into what there was of the dusty summit.

"Wow!" he exclaimed. "The view from up here is simply amazing" as he radioed down his first reaction to the others below. It was only several minutes before I and the other three joined Frederick on top of the dark black towering monolith.

We stood on the summit as a team, all amazed at the view of Phobos lit up in an orange hue reflection of the rusty planet Mars's daylight side. For the first time, humans have perched high above in the blackness surrounding them and could see more than sixty percent of this amazing potato-shaped small world.

Though we were five tiny-human specks in the grandiose size and existence of it all, we each felt a closeness to an unknown wonder of what our exploration would reveal once the three ships and crews reached our ultimate goal of mining 16-Psyche.

Jupiter, from here with the naked eye, was half the size of a full moon on Earth, and its four largest Galilean Moons were easily discernable as tiny stars that circled an orange-yellow-white globe that was engulfed by the blackness of space.

Alpha-1 from here was easily visible with its exterior silver color. Three of the six extended solar panels were reflecting our way from almost two miles away.

Bristol began the process of obtaining a core sample from the top of the monolith. As soon as the top two or three inches of dust and regolith were penetrated, his drill struck a hard surface and locked tight, causing his boots to release their grip and spinning him sideways.

Regaining his surface stance, Bristol reported that he was okay before he started to pull the shallow core sample up towards him. He seemed to be offering a pretty good resistance as he twisted the drill around in slow circles before it released its hold.

The core sample only accomplished five inches of depth, and at the very bottom of the three inches of regolith was about two inches of black hard coal-like substance that was hard enough to cause the drill to stop. I'll store this for later analysis once we return to Alpha-1. This entire monolith seems to be made of this exotic material Bristol Reported.

Shanta reported next. When I analyze it with my scanner, it registers as some sort of black molecular polymer consisting of thousands of thin layers that reveal each layer is bonded to the other with thousands of attach points.

"Its properties are similar to Velcro in cloth, except that this is an extremely hard polymer version. Whatever it is, it's incredibly lightweight and durable." Shanta said as she ended her report.

I stated that EVA excursion time is well over six and a half hours now. Let us store the sample and gear and prepare for our return to Alpha-1. They all agreed, and I, Jonathan, decided to plan the return in individual straight-line paths where we each would launch separately five minutes apart on our return one jump flight back to Alpha-1.

The space spring ejector boots had worked perfectly, and for the first time, I would attempt the one-step jump from the top of the monolith. Activated to provide a mile and a half jump, I rose up and soared gracefully from the high perch and my suit automatically engaged mini jets to auto guide my path back towards Alpha-1.

It was a fantastic slow flight that took approximately five minutes to complete. I was deeply amazed at the view. I felt like I was a seagull in a slow-motion glide path.

Somewhere in mid-flight, I was able to roll around and view the Mars terminator below as Phobos was almost at the point in its orbit of being eclipsed from sunlight by Mars. The view is beyond description of the Sun's rosy spectral colors reflected off of the edge of the thin Martian atmosphere.

After minutes of smooth flight, my vector changed, and suit jets rolled me around and began pushing me down slowly towards a point near Alpha-1. I touched the surface with a force that was no more than I jumped an inch high on Planet Earth. I only heard the immediate extraction swish sound from my boots as the four-inch curled claws secured my stance in a soft feet-first landing.

I was back, and after a quick look around, I radioed to the other four that all was clear for Shanta to begin her one-step flight return back to the safety of Alpha-1. Five minutes later, Shanta touched down a few meters away from where I was standing, and the others returned one at a time, five minutes apart.

We four watched as Frederick became the last to descend from his slow, easy approach. As soon as he landed, I gave the order to finish the activities in the immediate area and prepare to re-enter Alpha's compression hatch.

One by one, we all floated gracefully inside the hatch, and as I was the last to enter, the door slid closed and sealed behind me, and pressurized air began filling the cabin.

We rested in silence as the only sound now heard was the hissing of a nitrogen-oxygen atmosphere that took two minutes to pressurize to inside ship pressure.

CHAPTER 14

DAY-216 BRIEFING

In those silent moments, we five knew that we had just accomplished a mission to the base and very top of the monolith itself. We had photos of the strange encryption symbols at the bottom of the base and a small core sample from the top of the harmoniously tall rock that many scholars had wondered and pondered about for centuries.

Everyone inside wanted to know what the monolith's main structure was. Now with the core sample safely aboard the ship, the analysis could be conducted, and those unique properties may soon be revealed.

As a second egress process, we had to be decontaminated to prevent any foreign matter or unknown viruses from entering the ship. That process took several more minutes as we were all simultaneously bathed in bright ultraviolet spectral laser light to decontaminate any outside contaminates before being allowed to enter the inner section of Alpha-1.

Day-216 from launch, I, Captain Adams, began conducting my status briefing to the crew, and I instructed the crew to get to work on analyzing the monolith's core sample.

The number one priority at that time was to set our main objective for the next several days. The selection of the best landing location on Phobos for the Alpha-2 mining had yet to be determined.

Alpha-2 would be arriving in ten days, and there was no time to waste. I emphatically stated that I wanted a detailed report on the unique core sample properties obtained from the top of the monolith. We've got a lot of preparation to accomplish in order to be ready for the arrival of Alpha-2. Let's all get to work and get it done.

As soon as Alpha-2 has landed, the ship and crew will begin setting up and testing its mining capability on whatever site is selected. We need to all do our best to make sure that no mistakes are made in calculations and coordination.

"As your commander, you're a good crew, and I have extreme confidence in all on board. We can do this." I stated with certainty. "Let's concentrate our efforts and make this happen without incident or any more loss of life." Before ending the briefing, I reminded the crew that although Alpha-2 and 3 would only be sample mining of Phobos, It is not the primary goal of this mission to mine Phobos.

"Here on Phobos, the main intention is to test Alpha 2-and 3 in preparation for the intended mining journey to 16-Psyche. That's where the real treasure is expected to exist." After that statement, I ended my briefing, and the crew all floated away and departed to their station duties aboard Alpha-1.

Every crewmember was required to use the Earth Gravity Simulator Exercise Machines for at least an hour a day to keep their body muscles in shape. I would add time to their regular daily exercise schedule if any member got caught slacking in this extreme necessity. We were a dedicated crew, and we all complied studiously. We were humans. We indeed had to work hard at remaining human.

After a week of detailed analysis of the monolith core sample, I was issued a first analysis report on what technicians had learned.

It was very intriguing to learn that this material was constructed out of a super strong molecular black polymer that had never been discovered before. In the two-inch sample, more than a thousand separate layers had somehow been molecularly bound together to produce a lightweight polymer that acted like plastic-Velcro.

Each layer gripped the touching layer with many connection points that prevented each layer from sliding, and each layer bonded above and below tightly to the other. The monolith was entirely made out of a miraculous substance that we could not decide on whether it formed naturally or not. To our detailed analysis, it appeared to be created by intelligent design. Possibly the symbols upon deep study will allow for more detail in the future. The unique symbols were now in the process of being radioed to Mars base and then on to Earth for further analysis.

Captain Candice Roselle's Alpha-2 ship was now just 30 hours away from arrival, and the entire crew aboard was deeply engrossed in preparation for the upcoming landing.

A 5-members specialist team had decided on board that it was best to attempt to land Alpha-2 deep inside of Stickney Crater. That particular landing site deep inside Phobos could possibly reveal important facts about this small Moon that continuously races around Planet Mars.

It would be challenging to guide Alpha-2 to the floor level deep inside Stickney Crater. The real challenge would be to land near Limtoc Crater, which exists deep inside of Stickney Crater. It was determined that it was vital for Alpha-2's mining grinder to be able to sample the site that is closest to the center core of Phobos.

CHAPTER 15

ALPHA-2 LANDS ON PHOBOS

Twenty-eight hours later, the same five-exploration crew stood on a rocky creviced perch hanging over Stickney Crater's edge. Alpha-2 had matched Phobos's orbit and appeared in the distance as a flashing rotating spear above our heads. Occasionally you could make out a small thruster burst even as it was still over two kilometers above us. It descended closer by the minute, allowing better visual resolution, and in two minutes, the white round Pac-Man-looking craft was hovering 30 meters above the center of Stickney Crater.

We watched intensely as it descended past the edge performing a short reverse thrust to control its slow sinking depth inside the humongous Stickney Crater. Ever so slowly, Alpha-2 touched the surface a kilometer from Limtoc Crater and gave a two-second bounce before its grapple legs twisted and burrowed 12-inches into the surface.

Alpha-2 became invisible for several minutes while a slow settling cloud of dust obscured our view. We slapped suited hands together as a celebration as we could now begin to see the top of Alpha-2's control dome tower with the ship's lower part still surrounded by slow settling dust. We bounced back towards Alpha-1 excited to congratulate Captain Candice Roselle on her perfect landing.

CHAPTER 16
TESTING THE MINER

Within 24 hours, Alpha-2 was ready to begin its first test sample boring of the surface near Limtoc Crater. Alpha-2 on the surface appeared as a white half-ball shape with circular digging teethed rings around the bottom outside perimeter.

Alpha-2 had secured itself with four outer hydraulic powered legs and a main center pedestal ground attachment. When the order was given for the ring ejected metal teeth to eject and point downward, the teeth began spinning and slowly sinking as they began digging regolith. Alpha-2 began processing the matter it was capturing in the first meter of its depth and loading it on the center cargo pod.

After several hours of grinding, the rings stopped rotating as Alpha-2 had easily accomplished digging down to two-meters depth. Half mired in a cloud of Phobos matter, the inner works of the ship began analyzing and processing the matter that had been harvested and transporting it upward to the center cargo storage pod. The first few samples would be launched back to Earth for further analysis.

Alpha 2's first mining attempt was a big success. It was discovered that the micrometeorite contribution to the regolith of Phobos contained sufficient matter to coat the Moon with a layer of chondritic meteoritic material deep enough to obscure the underlying bedrock.

The bulk mineralogy by reflection spectroscopy or other surface matter analysis revealed that the meteoritic aerosol contribution from the atmosphere of Mars was significant and these particles could serve as condensation nuclei for the ice grains detected in the atmosphere by the Phobos-2 spacecraft that investigated Phobos over 200 years ago. Phobos didn't have any mining matter that would be worth long-term mining efforts. That was clear.

Drilling here on Phobos was only a test to reveal how the two mining digger ships would perform once we had reached our ultimate goal of 16-Psyche. No one had ever been there, but it was believed to contain many rare valuable resources such as titanium, gold, silver, and uranium. Who could possibly know what other precious metals we might find once we begin mining 16-Psyche?

We were then into Day-229 of our mission since departure from Gateway. Alpha-2 had successfully landed deep inside the 5.2-mile diameter Stickney Crater and was contentiously testing its equipment and operating a kilometer away from the edge of the 1.2 mile wide Limtoc Crater.

Limtoc was created by a long-ago cataclysmic crash that created another huge crater inside the much larger earlier infamous collision that created Stickney Crater.

On Day-234, all 40 members of both ships' crews gathered in the main counsel chambers aboard Alpha-1 to assimilate the briefing on the status of our mission to date. I, Captain Jonathan Adams, introduced Shanta and asked her to stand and give her report to all that were in attendance.

Shanta began, "We found the most abundant minerals to be Olivine (~90 wt%) and Pyroxene (~10 wt%)."

In this scenario, Phobos and Deimos would thus be very Olivine rich. Olivine and Pyroxene have characteristic absorption bands at 1 μm and 1 and 2 μm, respectively, that should be observed in the spectra of this moon.

This moon's featureless measured spectra by satellites reveal some interesting facts. Phobos' upper soil is extremely like Mars's soil. For eons, Mars has been shedding a trail-tail of dust and gasses, and Phobos seems to have wound up scooping some of the matter that has departed Planet Mars like a comet's tail over eons of time. She continued.

Meteors have bombarded Phobos for centuries, which is why the surface is covered in a meter of fine dust, mostly a very dark gray regolith that is not unconsolidated rocky debris. Phobos reflects only about 6 percent of the light falling on it, about one-half that of Earth's Moon.

Many of these charged particles that escape from Mars are ions of oxygen, carbon, nitrogen, and argon, and have been escaping Mars for billions of years while the planet has been shedding its atmosphere.

The report on the mining test for Alpha-2 revealed that the mining digger is working perfectly, and all is as it should be with Alpha-2's status. Shanta finished her report with a statement reporting that all is well with Alpha-3, and a different position near Gulliver Crater has been chosen for the landing site of Alpha-3 when it arrives in approximately six earth days. Shanta concluded that it's all so amazing and that more facts will be revealed when the first shipment is analyzed back on Earth.

I stepped to the podium and asked if anyone had any questions or concerns that needed to be discussed. Everyone seemed to be happy with all the details provided, and no one had any major concerns, so I adjourned the meeting with gratitude and confidence in the brave mining crew. We all had come so far in the first step of this daring mining expedition adventure.

CHAPTER 17

ALPHA-3 LANDS

Day-240 of the expedition. Captain Austin Williams had piloted Alpha-3 and acclimated the ship above the near side of Phobos's orbit. The Alpha-1 exploration team stood and watched as the blinking exterior lights came closer.

We watched intensely as six equal-spaced side jets slowed the approach of the round 750-feet diameter craft that now hovered about 150-meters above Gulliver Crater.

The ship stopped firing its sporadic thrusters and began silently sinking towards the center of Gulliver Crater. A meter above the surface, the ship excreted a final short blast through six nozzles before settling gently with a slight dusty bounce on the floor of Gulliver Crater.

Once Alpha-3 had settled from its bounce, it ejected from the bottom four legs with burrowing screw anchors that began drilling into the meter-thick dust and secured the ship inside Gulliver Crater.

On Day-242, Alpha-3 began its initial first test drilling inside Gulliver Crater. Its systems worked well, and analysis revealed much of the same results as Alpha-2's soil had revealed.

The mission was on schedule. The three ships and crew had arrived, and all were scheduled for a Day-260 launch towards their ultimate goal of leaving Phobos and journeying on as a team towards 16-Psyche.

The Psyche mission's plan was to leave Phobos on Day-260 because Mars was approaching conjunction on the inside orbit of Psyche. This was considered the best opportunity to launch towards 16-Psyche for the shortest possible travel time to their destination. Once launched, it would take the three ships five and a half months to arrive in the vicinity of 16 Psyche.

This dangerous mission we were about to undertake would require extreme caution, and if anything were to go wrong, there wouldn't be much chance for rescue this far out from Earth or Mars base.

On this journey, we would undoubtedly be on our own and only have each other to depend on. We were all aware of this fact, but we were a dedicated off-world mining crew determined to succeed in the greatest mining adventure ever attempted.

CHAPTER 18

DEPARTURE FROM PHOBOS

It was Day-259, and all was well thus far in our mission. Planet Mars was on Psyche's inside orbit, with its surface slowly receding from Phobos's outward, forward orbit.

For the past nine days, all three of the ship's crews had worked diligently together as a team to prepare Alpha-1 for the departure of Phobos, less than 23 hours away.

As head commander, I installed the computer command to program Alpha-1 to launch at the appropriate time of 0:800 on Day-260. Alpha-2 would launch 24 hours later on Day-261, and Alpha-3 would launch 24 hours after that on Day-262. Once all ships had departed Phobos, it would take 155 days to reach the vicinity of 16-Psyche in the asteroid belt.

None of the three Alpha ships were built for speed. These large mining vessels were designed to work well in low gravity environments.

These ships had much mass, and if you use extreme propulsion to speed up a large mass to a fast speed, you also have to use extreme fuel and opposite propulsion to slow down once you arrive at your destination. That's undeniable Physics.

These Alpha ships were only intended to achieve escape velocity from the Mars gravity well and gain just enough speed to reach Mars escape velocity and then coast most of the way to 16-Psyche.

It is possible that Alpha-1's engines had enough power to land on Mars had it become necessary, but Mars has only 38% of the Earth's gravity, and Phobos has less than .01% of Mars's gravity.

Alpha-2 and 3 only had the thrust capability to escape Phobos and Mars gravity well and land on light gravity bodies such as Phobos or other small heavenly bodies.

At 07:55 on Day-260, I, Captain Adams, gave the order to retract the screw anchors that attached Alpha-1's stability to the surface.

The engines were up and running. After verifying computer commands, I instructed the half-kilometer diameter ship to engage just enough thrust to achieve buoyancy and slowly rise from the Martian Moon Phobos. Alpha-1 seemed to fall slowly towards Mars below, and the ship soon obtained an altitude above Phobos of approximately 17 kilometers or 10 miles.

I directed Alpha-1 to make one loop around Phobos and fire slight thrusters to head towards the outside east leading edge of Mars's atmosphere. In 5 minutes, Alpha was skimming the eastern edge of Mar's orbital direction, and the gravity of Mars was causing our ship to curve in a loop around Mars.

Once we had approached three-quarters of the way around the planet, I engaged the engines to gain a speed of 6 kilometers or 3.2 miles per second to begin escaping the Mars gravity well.

Alpha-1 looped around Mars once and used the planet's gravity to slingshot the ship towards the direction vector that 16-Psyche would be in five and a half months from launch.

At our closest point, the ship was only 50 kilometers or 31 miles above Mars. It appeared as if we could easily reach down and touch the long Valles Marineris Chasm as Mars's gravity slung the ship around the backside of Mars and began moving silently away from Planet Mars.

I reported a speed of 6.2 kilometers per second as the ship's engines fell silent. That's the perfect speed required to enter behind Psyche and rendezvous in the asteroid belt once we arrive in five and a half months. Launch from Phobos was successful, and we were now on a glide path that the computer had analyzed and vectored Alpha-1 in the precise direction it needed.

Alpha-2 will be lifting off from Phobos in just under 23 hours. I then submitted the status report to the entire 27 other crewmembers aboard Alpha-1.

Shortly after Day-261 had begun, Alpha-2 had gently lifted above Phobos's surface, and when the ship had reached the required altitude, Alpha-2 circled Phobos once, and its engines guided the ship on a course that fell just in front of Mars's eastern atmospheric edge.

Captain Candice Roselle had piloted Alpha-2 and programmed its computers to slingshot around Mars for one close orbit while firing its engines three-fourths of the way behind Mars in order to accomplish the escape speed and launch it at 6.2 kilometers per second on a path directly following a day behind Alpha-1's trajectory towards 16-Psyche.

Day-262 Captain Austin Williams piloted Alpha-3 up and away from Phobos. He followed the same Mars slingshot maneuver that the other two ships used to acquire some of Planet Mars's gravity to launch towards a rendezvous with 16-Psyche.

518,400 kilometers or 322,118 miles separated each ship as the last Alpha ship departed Phobos and headed for the far away mysterious destination of 16-Psyche.

Communication at this distance only delayed two seconds between ships in each direction. This was way better than the 14-second delay each way that was experienced from Gateway to Phobos.

CHAPTER 19

SILENT CONVOY TO THE ASTEROID BELT

Separately but reasonably distanced apart, the three Alpha mining vessels sailed outward through the cold dark black void of space as the planet Mars now appeared as a penny-sized rusty-colored globe in the rear camera viewer. The three ship's outward vector would take us slightly above the ecliptic in order to arrive 24 million kilometers or 15 million miles above Psyche in the asteroid belt.

That high orbital approach above the asteroid belt was considered a cautious safety measure for these three Alpha ship crews that had ventured so far from Gateway Base that there was no possible chance of rescue should some catastrophic events occur.

The Asteroid belt itself is a very huge expanse. The asteroid belt is estimated to contain between 1.1 and 1.9 million asteroids larger than 1 kilometer or (0.6 miles) in diameter. There are millions of smaller ones there that orbit mostly eastward. An average distance of 5 to 10 million kilometers separates most of these larger asteroids, which is almost 15 times the distance between the Earth and the Moon.

If you consider the other asteroids, which are mostly the size of a small tennis ball, the relative distance between those would be way smaller.

The Psyche asteroid being 140.43 miles or 226 kilometers in diameter, was about 14 times larger than Phobos. But obviously, there are way larger objects in the belt other than this feeble metal asteroid as displayed below, with the largest being Ceres with a 588-mile or 946-kilometer diameter.

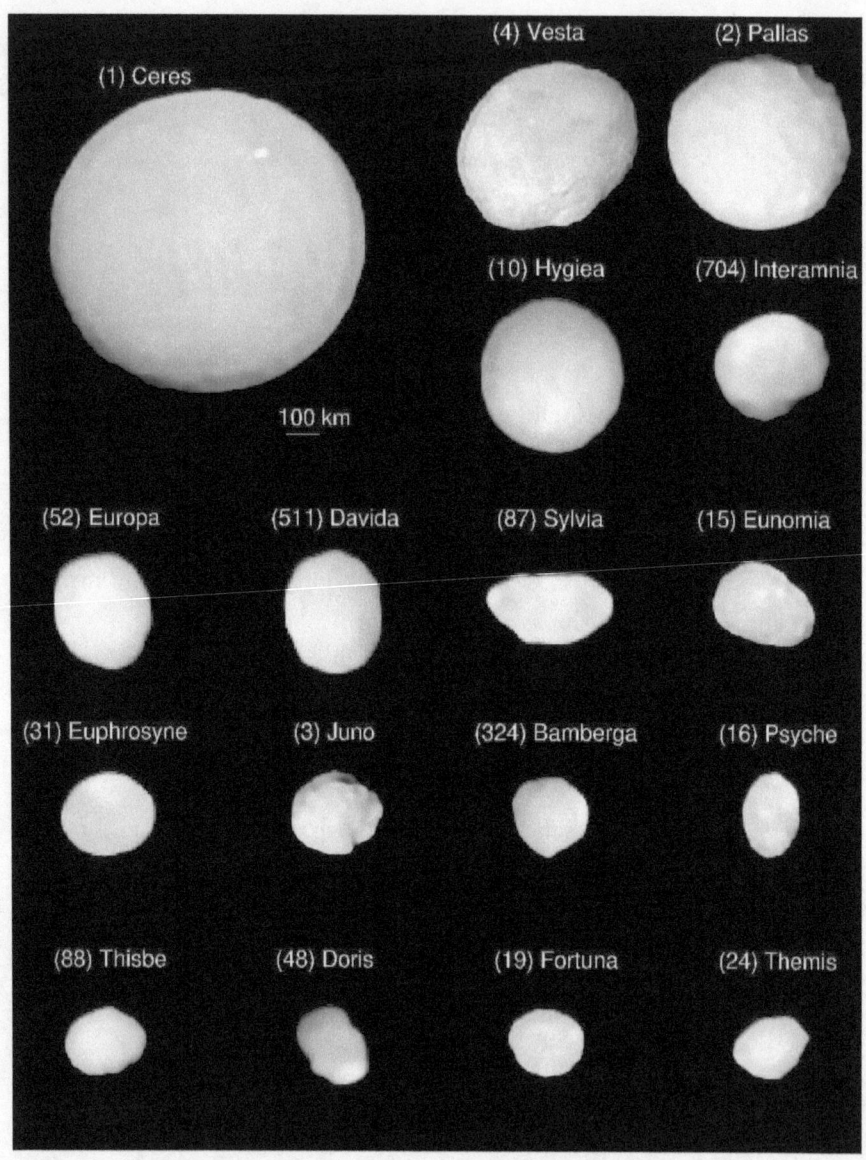

List of exceptional asteroids

These worlds were not the destination of our three-ship convoy. It was 16-Psyche or bust with us. The valuable metal retrieval of 16-Psyche was our ultimate goal. We sailed through the black void with diligence and assured confidence on Day-299. All three ships were scheduled to arrive above the vicinity of Psyche on Day-415, Day-416, and Day-417.

It is never like it has been portrayed in the many sci-fi movies of the past century. A ship could easily sail through the main asteroid belt with caution without being at the risk of getting hit by any asteroid.

We were on our way. This uniquely timed launch of the three ships away from Mars was intentionally used to allow the ships to catch up with Psyche from above the asteroid belt as it proceeded in its orbit. Psyche has an orbital speed around the Sun, approximately 17.34 kps or 10.77 miles per second.

All three of the Alpha ship's engines that left the vicinity of Mars at just over six kilometers per second were now engaged in continuous gradual thrust to slowly gain the speed of 16 kilometers or 10 miles per second relative to its orbit of the Sun in order to rendezvous high above Psyche in the asteroid belt on arrival beginning on Day-415. All seemed to be progressing well in our journey until a tragic occurrence on Day-361.

CHAPTER 20

TRAGEDY ABOARD ALPHA-2

At 03:14 AM on Day-361, an oblong meteor the size of a bus suddenly struck Captain Candice Roselle's Alpha-2 cataclysmically.

All communication was instantly lost after receiving a short non-comprehensible emergency signal. Very scare details were known about the ship's present status, but I, as Head Captain, had to take immediate action.

I, Captain Jonathan Adams, immediately dispatched four astronauts in two mini-shuttles to sojourn towards the location where Alpha-2 was last reported when the distress message was received. Alpha-3's Captain Austin Williams also dispatched one shuttle with two astronauts aboard to render aid if possible.

Specialist Josh Taylor along with Jessica Stone, piloted one of the Alpha-1's mini-shuttles while Inaner Mitchell and Ronald Howard piloted the second shuttlecraft to the rescue from Alpha 1.

From Alpha-3, astronauts Victoria Gulasky and Paul Hensley were also sent towards Alpha-2's last reported coordinates.

At top shuttle speed, the first two shuttles took less than an hour to arrive. Shocked eyes now focused on debris floating in all different directions around the dark remains of the Alpha-2 vessel.

Upon the first arrival, it was evident that this was a serious catastrophe. An entire side of Alpha-2 had been ripped away.

With no communication available, the survival of the ten aboard was presently unknown. Indeed if there were any survivors at all, something would have to be done to attempt a rescue.

An investigation by other means became the immediate priority of this rescue party. The observed damage was so extensive that it wasn't even possible to consider trying to dock with Alpha-2. Most of both docking modules on Alpha-2 had been ripped away in the collision.

The first known details were immediately reported back to Alpha-1 as the third smaller shuttle from Alpha 3 with Victoria Gulasky and Paul Hensley arrived on the scene.

CHAPTER 21

EVA-FLOATING RESCUE

Josh Taylor took immediate charge and calculated a rescue plan to attempt a two-person spacewalk to see if it was possible to enter the dark, damaged mining vessel and search for survivors.

In half hour's time, Josh Taylor and Ronald Howard were suited up and ready to enter the vacuum of space. After a few seconds, the depressurized cabin doors slid open, releasing the remaining air, and each floated away from their separate shuttles at the same time.

Both astronauts engaged their suit jets to propel towards the damaged half circle-ball dome on top of the apparent lifeless dark, jagged edges of Alpha-2.

To Josh and Ronald, the ship appeared as a huge broken white Pac-Man critter with jagged teeth hanging from its bottom where a huge bite was missing from its starboard side.

A three-minute silent glide through space vectored Josh towards a handrail on Alpha-2 as he grabbed it to stop his forward motion.

Ronald arrived at another handrail nearby 15 seconds after Josh. Both Astronauts immediately attached a temporary tether to their handrails. Josh radioed to Ronald that they should ease around to the still intact side to see if it was possible to enter an excursion hatch on the far side of Alpha-2.

"Okay," Ronald replied. "You go first, and I'll follow close behind." Josh released his tether, activated soft control jets, and vectored slowly through space around to where a mining excretion port was still intact and soon followed by Ronald.

"We should be able to enter this extraction chamber doorway here," Josh radioed to Ronald. "Acknowledged," Ronald replied as he glided towards a locker positioned beside two double rectangular doors.

"These doors can be opened manually," Ronald said as he opened the outer storage cabinet. "There's a T-crank tool in here that fits into that gear on the door's lower side. That should allow us access to the inner mining chamber station."

Ronald opened the cabinet and retrieved the T-shaped meter-length metal tool. He then pushed away and floated towards the gear below and at the center of the double doors. He planted his magnetic boots directly below the 12-inch gear.

"It's extremely cold," Josh radioed to Ronald. "It will take both of us to break it free so that it will turn." Josh landed beside Ronald while inserting the crank tool into the slotted gear. Each grabbed an end of the T-Crank and pushed with all of their mass, but the gear was frozen solid.

"This is not working," Josh radioed to Ronald.

"You should float back away a bit." Josh insisted.

"I'm going to brace myself backward and position one of my backpack jets directly over the stuck gear and ignite it while I attach my magnetic boots to the side of the ship. The flame from the thruster should heat the gear and possibly free it up so it can be turned."

"That's a good plan," Ronald replied. "I'll be ready to jump in with the T-wrench as soon as you've released your magnetic boots and move out of the way."

"Okay," Josh replied.

"I'll heat the gear for sixty seconds, and as soon as I release, I'll spin around and come right back to help you put force and twist the gear while it's still hot."

"Sounds like a great plan," Ronald replied as Josh was presently in the progress of locking himself above the gear with his center backpack's jet facing a foot above the frosty gear.

Josh was able to lock his magnetic boots while squatting backward and getting the propulsion nozzle to within six inches of the frozen gear.

Ronald watched as the flame ignited.

"Move six inches to your right," Ronald suggested.

"Stop right there!" Ronald injected as he watched Josh restrain his locked knees against the propulsion of the flame's jet.

Ronald began tightly holding on to Josh's backpack and began visually focusing the hot stream directly over the gear cog while rolling the backpack's flame slowly around in circles between the cog's teeth.

A slow six circles of heat between the gear's teeth and Ronald quickly let go of Josh and grabbed the T-shaped tool from his tool belt as Josh released his boot locks against the ship and spun around once in 10 seconds, locking right back beside Ronald that had already inserted the tool into the heated gear.

Each grabbed a side of the T-bar as Josh shouted, turn it counter-clockwise. Josh began straining and pushing hard while Ronald applied his strength towards pulling on the meter-long T-bar.

The gear suddenly broke free and turned. They were able to twist three revolutions of the T-bar that accomplished an entry opening of about 48 inches.

They floated silently up through the opening and crossed an airless storage bay into the dark interior of Alpha-2's wreckage. They landed beside a sealed doorway.

"It's partially pressurized inside," Josh radioed while reading the inside pressure gauge on the outside wall.

Ronald placed his helmet against a foot-diameter bubble window and focused his vision on what he could see inside.

"Hey, wait!" he exclaimed

"I can see two people floating inside. They are in spacesuits but not aware of us yet."

Ronald took a small metal tool and lightly tapped upon the small bubble window. The tapping sound could not get their attention because there was very little air pressure inside to carry sound waves. Ronald projected his helmet light through the glass to alert the survivors to their presence.

The two inside floated forward and began frantically trying to communicate through hand gestures. They scribbled a message on a card.

"*Calvin Stubs - Alee Dempsey - air supply low*," was the message written upon the message card.

Josh took out a marker, scribbled his reply on his suit sleeve, and held it close to the window for both to see.

"Attach tethers to the wall. I will break the glass and release the remaining pressure to allow the door open."

They both nodded their helmets and floated smoothly across to a far side storage compartment and retrieved two tethers available inside. Each fastened their tethers to the inside far wall struts and separated them by about sixteen feet. Both gave a thumbs-up signal towards the window.

"You'd better move away about 10 meters," Josh radioed Ronald. "I'm going to burst this pressurized glass window with the pointed end of my rock hammer, and glass is going to spew out fast."

Josh had a pointed rock hammer that would weigh 5 pounds on earth. He braced himself and swung a right-handed force towards the center of the bubble window. Instantly, with no sound, an outward explosive force blasted shards of debris above his head. Glass and paper debris ejected into space until the air pressure inside had become a total vacuum. The tethers had prevented Stubs and Dempsey from being injured, but the door still didn't want to open.

Both astronauts attached magnetic boots beside the door and pulled as hard as they could. The door finally released its frozen seal and slid open. They found Studs and Dempsey floating and attached to their tethers. Their suits had been damaged, with very little electrical power and oxygen left in their backpacks.

Ronald tethered to one and Josh to the other, and the astronauts began towing the two survivors out of the ship and back towards their separate shuttles a half kilometer away through the dark void of space.

Each loaded their survivor aboard, and both shuttles engaged thrusters to return as fast as possible to Alpha-1. The third smaller shuttle crew, Victoria Gulasky and Paul Hensley, also left the area and headed back towards Alpha-3.

Josh and Ronald entered emergency codes into their ship's computers, and each shuttle engaged full thrust to arrive back at Alpha-1 as soon as possible. The survivor on each shuttle was barely conscious, and their medical status was critical.

In 45 minutes, both shuttles had used most of their fuel supply and managed to dock to Alpha-1. The survivors were immediately rushed to the medical facility aboard Alpha-1.

The expedition had now lost two souls aboard Alpha-1 and eight aboard Alpha-2. The two survivors would recover, but each told of a frightening experience. An unknown object had collided and destroyed their ship. They both told a horrifying tale of how they managed to survive.

Alpha-2 was no longer a working machine, but it was decided that Alpha-3 would attach to it and tow the remains towards 16-Psyche in case any of the parts could be salvaged.

Day-361 and Day-362 had been tragic times for the once three-ship expedition. Now we journeyed on as a two-ship rendition of what we once were. Having lost a total of ten crewmembers along our journey, we had a major decision to be made. Should we continue, or should we turn around and retreat towards Mars Base?

Day-364 became a day for honoring the souls lost along our journey. A ceremony was held and a single simulation casket was ejected with a memorial inside to honor our fallen heroes. There had been no hope of rescuing the other eight bodies that were blasted into space. Any human that wasn't in a spacesuit when the collision tragedy occurred succumbed instantly to the cold airless vacuum. The two that were rescued just happened to be suiting up for an EVA when the collision occurred.

CHAPTER 22
VOTE TO CONTINUE

Head Captain Jonathan Adams called a ship-wide emergency conference with all aboard linked visually. At the same time, Alpha-3's crew was also linked to the meeting by video link with a 5-second delay due to the distance between ships.

Captain Austin Williams has reported that Alpha-3 has accomplished catching up with the remains of Alpha-2 and was now towing the destroyed vessel a few days' travel distance behind Alpha-1.

After that brief report, Captain Adams spoke to the remaining 39 others on the mission. I know it's been hard on us all I said. We've all endured a tremendous setback. We're 50-days away from 16-Psyche, and at this point, we have a critical decision to make. In My opinion, We still have good options left. But this far along the mission, I've decided that the decision to carry on should be left up to the rest of you in a democratic vote on whether to proceed to 16-Psyche or return to Mars Base.

With 39 crewmembers beside myself, I will leave this decision to the votes of the 39 others, not including myself. There is no possibility of a tie with 39 members voting.

This is such an important decision that I order all crew members to vote within an hour of the end of this briefing. The majority vote of 39 members will control our destination. The vote in question is *yes* equals continue, and *no* equals return home. It's your decision.

Every member is required to vote within one hour from the end of this conference to prevent any possibility of a tie. That's an immediate order that I, Jonathan Adams, state emphatically. You must all vote. This emergency conference has ended and will reconvene in one hour when the votes are tabulated.

Captain Adams reconvened the meeting in an hour, and the vote was revealed. You've all voted to continue the mission, he reported. Just let me express my pride in every crew member. We shall continue, and if I had voted, I would have voted to continue also.

Just let me say this Captain Adams spoke briefly over the video link. Baring any other catastrophe, We still have the Alpha-3 mining ship, and parts may be scavenged from Alpha-2 if needed. Although our mining capability potential has decreased, we can still mine 16-Psyche and gain some of its rewards, but we must endure our loss and work as a team to succeed. Captain Jonathan Adams signed off to all of the crews, and the conference ended.

The tragedy of the past few days had been hard on both of the ship's crew. Crewmembers had lost close long-time friends and one member had lost her husband. But the crew managed to knuckle down and somehow remain sane on this far-away adventure. Some had reasons for wanting to give up and return home, but close friendship ties helped to resolve most doubts.

We sojourned onward with our hearts and minds dwelling on the possible riches we could gain in mining 16-Psyche. Things went along smoothly for the next month as the ship began climbing high above the edge of the asteroid belt.

On Day-399, the 39 crewmembers gathered around the monitors to hear and assimilate Captain Adams's broadcast on the two ship's present status. All members paid strict attention to the broadcast as I began speaking.

I'm calling you today to inform both ships' crews of our present status. Alpha-3 is successfully towing the remains of Alpha-2, but due to the extra mass it is pulling, it has had to slow down and change its course slightly and, therefore, should arrive behind us in about six more days instead of the two-day delay that was planned.

I'm aware that everyone knows that Alpha-1 is only 16 Earth Days away from arriving in the vicinity of Psyche. Once we land and get set up, as a team, we will have to figure a way to help Alpha-3 place Alpha-2's remains in a safe stable orbit not too far behind Psyche's orbital path before Alpha-3 can attempt to land on Psyche.

Once we succeed in securing Alpha-2's remains behind Psyche's orbital path, this expedition will have access to Alpha-2 parts for Alpha-3 should it become necessary.

I've ordered a team of three volunteers to immediately get busy computing the calculations that Captain Austin Williams will need to place the remains of Alpha-2 in a stable orbit behind Psyche's orbital path.

I want another team of three to calculate the specific approach and landing coordinance that Melissa and I will require in order to land on 16-Psyche safely.

Once we are two days away, we'll make a first-choice decision on the best place to land. That's all I have for now. I know that all of you will do your best; with your help, Melissa and I can do ours. This is Captain Jonathan Adams signing off until we are forty-eight hours away from 16-Psyche.

By Day-412, both teams had worked diligently to accomplish the Captain's orders. Although delayed while towing Alpha-2, Alpha-3 was still making good progress towards our destination.

Early on Day-413, both crews gathered around the video monitors to hear Captain Adam's status report. His demeanor assured the crews that Alpha-1 was in good shape and ready to pick the ship's landing spot on 16-Psyche. Captain Adams began his report with a present known Psyche facts report.

CHAPTER 23

16 PSYCHE FACTS

16-Psyche is a very strange M-class asteroid. The asteroid appears potato-shaped and has a mean diameter of approximately 220 kilometers or 140 miles. Psyche contains about one percent of the mass of the entire asteroid belt. This asteroid is more reflective than anything else in the asteroid belt between Mars and Jupiter. It is so bright that it's presumed to be composed mainly of metals. I can't be specific, but it is assumed to contain many valuable assets such as uranium, titanium, nickel, iron, gold, and many other rare minerals.

Mine-X Corporation has estimated that it could be worth about 10,000 quadrillion dollars. Recent studies have revealed that it may even be more valuable than the estimate I quoted. That is why it is such a high priority for this asteroid mining expedition. That is why we are here.

Captain Adams continues his report to the crews. Our navigation crew has determined that the best place to land on Psyche is near a crater called *Charlie Crater*. This crater is at zero degrees latitude on the Psyche equator.

Psyche completes one rotation every 4.2 earth hours. It will be much easier to match its rotation rate and safer to land at Charlie Crater since it is directly on the equator.

We can always relocate the ship if necessary after exploring different areas on the asteroid. It takes approximately five Earth Years for Psyche to orbit the Sun once. That's a 16-Psyche year.

Once set up on the surface, our mission stay is scheduled to be five earth years, depending on what we can mine there. Each future relief crew will serve a term of one Psyche year.

If all goes well as the mission continues, a relief crew and another digger ship will arrive here in just over three years. Any member wishing to return home at that time will definitely be allowed to do so.

We're two days away from landing. I personally depend on all aboard Alpha-1 to help me meet the challenge of safely landing this ship. Captain Adams signing off.

CHAPTER 24
ALPHA-1 LANDS ON PSYCHE

There was a serene view out of the starboard window as Alpha-1 soared above a portion of the sun reflecting section of the asteroid belt. Ceres from here was the size of a marble and visible way behind the ship's vector floating in the middle of thousands of other ice sparkling smaller asteroids all headed in the same curved direction around the Sun.

Alpha-1 was now 20 hours away from arriving above Psyche's orbital track that was already locked into the ship's radar. Over the next few hours, the ship was vectoring in a downward curve to approach above Psyche as the speed was equaled. A telescopic visual of the metal asteroid revealed the rotation rate of Psyche's once every 4.7-hour spin.

Psyche is an oval potato-shaped asteroid with Charlie Crater prominent on its eastern edge. Its diameter is approximately 225 by 193 kilometers or 140 by 120 miles.

If you think of an oval potato shape on its side, supported at the bottom at a center rotation point, turning once in its orbital direction every four hours and 49 minutes, that would be the way that Psyche orbits the Sun in the asteroid belt.

Two hours from touchdown, Alpha-1 had descended from above the asteroid belt, and telescopic visual and radar lock was directing the ship downward towards the approaching asteroid of metal. As minutes passed, Alpha-1 sank closer to the rotating metallic world below.

Alpha-1 matched Psyche's orbital path and then began matching Psyche's rotation rate to approach the zero-degree equatorial coordinance where Charlie Crater was located.

As Alpha-1 matched the exact rotation rate in orbit, a visual of Charlie Crater at one-kilometer altitude was displayed below the ship and on the monitor. Ever so slowly, Alpha-1 used reverse repulsion to allow the ship to descend at a speed of 10 feet per second. In five and a half minutes, Alpha-1 now emitted slight propulsion as it hovered three meters above the surface of Charlie Crater.

The Octagon shaped Alpha-1 descended gently and bounced slightly, touching the surface with very little dust being disturbed. Immediately after touchdown, ships hydraulic anchors were attempted to deploy to secure the ship to the surface.

Alpha-1 had landed. The view out of the portals revealed a world like no human had ever experienced before. In the two hours 22 minutes on the sun-lit side, reflections off the surface revealed colorful properties and moving shadows as Psyche rotated along its orbital path.

The surface temperature on the sunlit side was a surprising 25 degrees Fahrenheit or -3.8 Celsius. We had only a 35-minute view of the colorful reflected metal surface before Psyche's shadowy darkening dusk rolled around to its 2.2-hour night with -150 degrees Fahrenheit or -101.1 Celsius.

We became enhanced with the beauty of the outer solar system surrounded by vivid starlit darkness around Jupiter with four reflecting moons bouncing reflected solar light our way.

Captain Adams issued a short happy statement that all on board understood. If only Annibale de Gasparis could see what we see. We indeed have arrived. Congratulations Crew. Tomorrow we begin exploration. Captain Adams out.

Day-416

CHAPTER 25
FIRST PSYCHE EVA

Captain Adams, Fredrick Crews, and Melissa Harper suited up in the ready room to perform the first outside EVA. It was decided that only three would perform the first EVA as a precautionary measure in case something went wrong. They were used to light gravity, and Psyche's gravity was five times stronger than the almost zero gravity of Phobos. The gravity weight of a suited astronaut was still less than 10 ounces on the surface of Psyche.

Psyche was experiencing its early dawn when the cabin door swished open the remainder of air pressure to the outside. A Purple hazy sky lit the leading edge in their view as the asteroid began its two-point two-hour sun-facing day. Tall jagged shadows from an easterly peak reflected on an even darker thin dusty soil that swallowed more shadows as they intermingled in retreat.

Melissa Harper gave a slight spring push from her boots, sailed out the door, and gently settled 10 feet outside the hatch door. Frederic Crews went next. Then Captain Adams settled behind him 15 seconds later. Melissa used her tricorder to analyze the surrounding area and then reported the readings. My reading shows Psyche is 82.5% metal, 7% low-iron pyroxene that are rock-forming minerals, and 10.5% carbonaceous chondritic or stony material.

Its bulk density, or porosity, is around 5%. I'm registering many different kinds of rare metals. Gold, platinum, nickel, silver, iron, and many more medals are registering on my laser tricorder. There is an area near *West Alpha Crater* 140 kilometers towards the west that, even from this distance, is read to be made of pure platinum, gold, and silver.

There is one more reading of an unknown metal type that the tricorder can not identify. Melissa ended her report with a statement saying that we'll have to wait until Alpha-3 is set up and operational to determine what that unknown medal is.

Bravo was the most enormous crater on Psyche. Our first sojourn was to investigate *Bravo Crater*, which measures 33 miles or 53 kilometers in diameter and 4 miles or 6.4 kilometers deep.

"We're first going to explore Foxtrot Crater." Captain Adams spoke up. "My best estimate is that it's about 8 kilometers distance from here. We can use the spring boots and suit jets to get us to the edge in about 10 minutes if we energize our boot spring launches to about a kilometers distance with each jump."

"We need to use caution." the Captain stated. "This surface out here only has a thin layer of dust on top, and there is not much for the grips on our boots to dig into."

Psyche was reaching its mid-day rotation when the three-headed off on a bounding flight path northward towards *Foxtrot Crater*. This huge crater was very near Psyche's North Pole rotation point.

On our sixth flight jump, we landed gently near a high crevice looking down into the 33-mile diameter Foxtrot Crater, whose rock surface glistened with a spectrum that could only register visually as pure gold.

"Wow!" Melissa exclaimed. "Look down along the floors inside the crater splash. There's a vain of purple-red diamonds that circle the entire floor all along the outer edge of the once molten metal matter."

"There's also a lot of pure iron content registering," Melissa stated. "It looks like Psyche indeed has a lot of rare Earth minerals and is not as porous as a scientist of the 21st century had predicted. Psyche was no rubble pile of rocks that had coalesced into an asteroid. Psyche must be the inner metal core of a used-to-be planetoid that existed in the asteroid belt. Eons ago, it had its crust blown away by some cataclysmic collision."

"Perhaps even Ceres once was a moon of this remaining metal core that we call 16-Psyche. Possibly all of the matter that makes up the asteroid belt was the remains of the outer surface matter that once encased Psyche's metal core. "

"Maybe so," Frederick gave his response to Melissa's postulation. "Something cataclysmic surely happened in this asteroid belt many eons ago. We may never learn the actual facts of Psyche's history. For certain, it is indisputable that Psyche is the metal core of a long-ago planetoid that existed here in the center of Mars and Jupiter's orbit around the Sun."

"That's all very debatable," Jonathan Adams spoke up. "We're more than 50 kilometers away from Alpha-1, and Psyche will enter its night cycle in approximately 20 minutes. Since this is our first exploration EVA, we should stay cautious and head back to the ship before sunset."

With those words, Jonathan loaded his boot spring launcher, arose from the surface, and headed toward Alpha-1's safety. Within 15 minutes, they were all back at Alpha-1 and preparing to enter the ship.

Jonathan was the last to enter the hatch, and he paused a moment to take in the view of the sinking setting sun as it cast long crusty shadows across the hatch door. A sudden frosty temperature change instantly activated the heaters inside all three of their spacesuits. Pressurization began immediately as Captain Adams activated a switch that closed, sealed, and locked the cabin door. On their first exploration excursion outside the ship, it was considered a safety issue not to be outside during the two-hour Psyche night period.

Their spacesuits were very capable of withstanding the low temperatures on the night side of Psyche. Caution was used because this had been the first EVA to venture outside the ship's immediate vicinity since landing a day earlier.

Their spacesuits had performed perfectly as designed, and the super magnetic enhancers added to their boots helped the astronauts a great deal on this highly metal orbiting asteroid.

With many future days of exploration ahead, these spacesuits would surely be tested, especially when Alpha-3 arrives and begins its mining operation in four earth rotation periods.

Day-419

Several sojourns of exploration had occurred over the next two days. *Meroe, Bravo, Golf, India,* and *Delta Craters* were explored. After much research, it was decided that the huge crater named Foxtrot would be the chosen site for Alpha-3's landing in two earth rotation periods.

On Day-420, a special team aboard Alpha-1 had engineered the precise coordinance that Alpha-3 would require in order to place the remains of Alpha-2 behind Psyche's exact orbital path and speed around the Sun.

The asteroid belt was a very peaceful place once you traveled at the speed of all the rocks and pebbles that live there. Everything traveled at the same basic speed and on an easterly directional path. Once Alpha-2 is positioned behind Psyche's orbit, it will be easy to access should parts be needed for Alpha-3.

Day-421

CHAPTER 26

ALPHA-2'S STORAGE ORBIT

Radar was locked in on Alpha-3's approach, but communication had been blocked every time the body of Psyche shielded the signal by entering its two-hour night.

Twelve hours before arrival, a gyrosyncronous satellite was launched from Alpha-1. That allowed continuous last-minute communication as Alpha-3 approached while towing Alpha 2's remains with a 750-meter long tether.

Alpha-3 sank lower behind the rotating Psyche and continued to decrease the asteroid's lead by gently using thrust to approach the precise speed and release point for Alpha-2's orbit. It took an hour for Alpha-3 to slowly descend to within 400 kilometers or 248 miles behind 16-Psyche.

Several hours earlier, four astronauts from Alpha-3 had installed control thrusters on the remains of Alpha-2 so that it could be controlled remotely from Alpha-1 Base once released from Alpha-3.

All aboard, both vessels watched intently as the monitor view showed Alpha-3 reaching the perfect orbital release point. The long tether disengaged from Alpha-2 and slowly began retracting into Alpha-3's cargo storage bay. Within 15-minutes, the retraction had finished. From Alpha-1 control, the mini thrusters that were installed on Alpha-2 were activated and pushed the wreckage another half kilometer Away from Alpha-3.

CHAPTER 27

ALPHA-3 LANDS IN FOXTROT CRATER

With the Alpha-2 wreckage placement accomplished, Alpha-3 began using engine thrust to catch up to Psyche and started its final orbital maneuver in order to match up with Psyche's fast rotation speed. It was extremely necessary to match Psyche's rotation speed before any ship could possibly land on this asteroid or any other asteroid.

The 750-meter diameter mining craft hovered two kilometers over the center of the 33-mile diameter and 4-mile deep Foxtrot Crater. Retro decreased, and Alpha-3 slowly sank below the crater's peak and hovered for 15 seconds. Gradually sinking lower, in several short minutes, Alpha-3 again hovered 30 meters above its targeted landing intention.

For the last 45 seconds, the ship floated downward as light as a feather and bounced slightly before four-legged anchors unfolded and attempted to engage the surface to hold the ship tight to Psyche's low gravity surface. The surface was so metallic-hard that the anchors were unable to penetrate only 3 centimeters into the thin layer of Psyche regolith dust.

Both crews let out a celebrated yell as the news of Alpha-3's landing instantly echoed through the ranks. We had accomplished our goals new beginning. All was well, and anticipation of this brave mining attempt reminded us why we were here. Now it was reality.

Yes, we had suffered loss along the way, but somehow we all managed to pull together to salvage what we could by choosing to venture on after tragic loss. With determination, we continued the mission that many had said was impossible.

Three Alpha vessels and fifty dedicated crewmembers had now proved to everyone back on Earth that it could be done, and we as a team did it. We were on Psyche and ready to go to work. The Day-421 celebration party lasted until midnight, and all 40 surviving members celebrated their grand achievement.

On Day-422, Alpha-1's priorities were to retract its anchors and move Alpha base closer to Alpha-3 above the rim of Foxtrot Crater. It was virtually as easy to move Alpha's half-kilometer diameter mass as it was for a single astronaut to sail above the surface. Alpha-1 base now settled easily on a flat surface very close to the edge of Foxtrot Crater.

A suited astronaut could quickly jump from the crater's edge and gradually sink the 4 miles depth to the floor below without being harmed. Even in a spacesuit, an astronaut would only weigh approximately 8 or 9 ounces on Psyche. It was also easy to jump out of Foxtrot Crater and land back at Alpha-1 Base.

On Day-423, Alpha-3 began the operation of the mining process at the bottom of Foxtrot Crater. Four astronauts stood a kilometer away at the bottom of Foxtrot as the bottom outer blades began rotating while shooting sparks as the light gravity surface resisted the diamond blades' drilling attempt. After a dozen rotations, the ship started losing its grip and bounced a meter high as the rotation seized, and the ship settled down to the metal surface again.

The test drilling immediately stopped, and we four sailed a kilometer distance; and in 60 seconds, we landed near Alpha-3.

Alpha 3's four anchor screws had only penetrated the hard metal surface about a half-inch deep. The main center hydraulic support was also the same, and the mining ship could not pull downward with enough force so that the blades could put grind into the surface.

A solution had been anticipated in the early mission planning stage. The solution would require astronauts to melt the surface below each of Alpha's five hydraulic anchors, press an anchor insert receptor into the molten rock, and then allow the matter to cool. This required work would take several days for teams of astronauts to sink all five anchors one sortie at a time.

CHAPTER 28
SINKING THE ANCHORS

Day-424 began with the tasks of getting the necessary equipment together for tomorrow's start of sinking Alpha 3's main center anchor. The laser had to be transported to the base of Alpha-3 from Alpha-1 above.

A working team of four astronauts floated over the rim's edge and sank downward towards Alpha-3. Four opposing gloved hands were gripped tightly to the forward momentum mass of the open framed 2-meter tall caged laser platform. Everything bounced slightly as the transporters settled the laser's mass to the surface ten meters away from Alpha-3.

Alpha-3's inside crew was in the process of retracting its center hydraulic support as the astronauts landed and waited for the support to retract a meter above helmet head height completely. Once retracted, a team of four lifted the laser and placed it directly below Alpha's center support structure.

Two astronauts began attaching a pointed half-meter length round threaded anchor sinker on the bottom of the retracted center support. The threaded anchor insert is designed to allow twisted insertion inside a female threaded receiver pipe once it is installed and cooled.

The receiver pipe will be sunk into the molten matter and allowed to cool and harden around the insert. This would enable the ship's attached hydraulic threaded anchor supports to screw inside of the attached surface receptor once the matter around each receptor sleeve has cooled.

These anchor sleeves were necessary to allow the ship's anchors to pull downward while cut mining and then be unscrewed when moving Alpha-3 to another location. The anchor sleeve sinking detail would be required each time the ship was relocated.

With the female attachment insert connected to the retracted pedestal overhead, the laser was placed below the pedestal and connected to Alpha 3's nuclear power source.

From four corners of the upside-down bowl Pac-Man-shaped ship, astronauts watched through protection shields as the bright laser activated and began heating a 14-inch diameter circle below the ship. Sparks from the surface bounced at an angle high into space in the low gravity. A circular thin molten mass began to form beneath the laser's torched flame.

The high-powered laser took about 15 minutes to penetrate twelve inches deep. Power was increased to maximum, and it took almost another hour to melt the insert pool down to a half-meter depth.

A 14-inch circle of molten metal now boiled beneath the ship as the laser deactivated and the pivot arm brace swung the laser out of the way. The ship's center support began slowly pressing the 10-inch diameter steel female inside-threaded insert into the molten pit that the laser had just melted.

Once the top of the insert was pressed down to six inches above being flush with Psyche's surface, the insert was released and allowed to cool for an hour before the ship's male outer threaded center support began connecting with slow clockwise rotations.

A slow rotation of the ship's center outer threaded hydraulic support was attached to the inner threads of the female receiver insert, and the motion stopped when the threaded connection was complete.

Liquid hydrogen was injected inside the center connection tube to speed up the cooling of the receiver sleeve. This allowed the matter around the receiver pipe to complete its cooling process once the connection was attached to the sleeve insert.

Bent-light heat waves were being emitted above the cooling insert, and Psyche's dusk was about to drop the surface temperature to minus

150 degrees Fahrenheit. The sunken anchor would be allowed to cool for 24 hours before Alpha-3 would finalize tightening the threads to obtain a firm grip on the low gravity Psyche world.

This first work EVA had lasted six hours and sinking the four outer spider leg supports would each require a work EVA of their own. In order to sink the anchor sleeves at each of the outside four hydraulic spider-like legs, it would require days of hard work to accomplish all five supports to be anchored down. These were hard-working miners. No one in this crew ever thought that mining a faraway asteroid would be easy. Indeed it is not.

This anchor mounting work was necessary because of the hard metal surface and extremely light gravity of 16 Psyche. The mining ship's pull-down bite on the surface had to be hydraulically computer equalized at all five points of the force that the ship's grinding teeth could apply to the surface.

This precise pull would allow the rotating laser blasting cutting teeth to be pressed hydraulically downward while its jagged diamond blade laser teeth heated and allowed ingestion of the molten mined matter.

Each cutting tooth projected a laser at its point. The laser enabled the softening of matter as the bottom ring blades scooped and forced the cut matter upward into the top of the center-launch pod container.

Psyche had exposed the cooling matter around the sleeve insert for 5 of its cold night rotations or one earth day's time. Captain Austin Williams issued the go-ahead from the Alpha base and began lowering its center screw head support slowly downward toward the insert installed on Day-426.

The ten-inch threaded support rod touched the insert and began rotating slowly clockwise to the right as the threads caught hold and, in a few minutes, had accomplished screwing into the threaded insert six inches and locked to a stop.

For the first time now, the Alpha-3 digger ship was firmly attached to the surface of Psyche.

Day-428 thru Day-431 were spent working toward connecting each of the four outer legs of Alpha-3 to the surface with sunken steel anchors sleeves so that each leg could be screwed to the anchor when cooled and to the surface like the center support was attached.

Alpha-3's legs were spread out past the edge. The hydraulic-powered rotating blades, the center-connected support, and the four braced legs were able to pull the ship's circular cutting blades downward with equal pressure as the rotating blades began cutting and processing the hard surface matter below Alpha-3.

Day-431

CHAPTER 29

PSYCHE MINING BEGINS

Captain Austin Williams activated the rotation of Alpha's 750-feet diameter circular cutting blades.

The rotating outer cutting ring chamber was equipped with 360-degree lasers in front of each cutting tooth blade. Each laser would fire a blast every second to soften the mass that was being cut-mined. When heated, the matter was much easier to cut with the diamond tip blades.

The metals on Psyche were so hard that it took 30 mining days for Alpha-3 to cut down to a half-meters depth, even when heated. In this light gravity, the matter that was mined was easily channeled upward through tubes and funneled into an available 10-meter tall 3-meter diameter earth return cargo cylinder.

Eleven more empty cargo pods stood waiting to be loaded, but after the first 30-days of tough Psyche mining, Alpha-3 had only produced enough matter to fill 50 percent of one container. Alpha-3 was only able to cut down to a depth of 2-meters, and the remaining meter and a half mining process would take several more months to be completed.

Once the 2-meter cutting depth is accomplished, the ship must release the five anchors and move Alpha-3 to a different mining location. New anchor inserts were required for each site that was mined.

CHAPTER 30

FIRST CARGO POD LAUNCHED TO EARTH

Much progress and dedicated preparation had been accomplished, and on Day-491, a single cargo storage cylinder had been filled and was ready to be launched to Earth. Once launched, the pod was equipped with remotely controllable ion guidance engines capable of sailing it back towards Earth so that Mine-X Corporation could capture the pod in Earth orbit.

The Alpha-3 mining ship had functioned exceptionally well, and now the first of its twelve cargo cylinders were loaded with the processed matter gained in the past from Foxtrot Crater.

On the very top of Alpha-3, a five-meter diameter circular double-door opened above the loaded cargo cylinder. The launch timer counted down to zero when Ion pulsed rockets ignited and lifted the cylinder silently through the opening above. At first, the container rose a half-meter per second, and in 20 seconds, the tail of the cargo rocket had escaped the confines of Alpha-3's launch door.

In another half-minute, the cylinder had obtained half a kilometer altitude when stronger pulsed rocket thrust ignited and began pushing the cargo cylinder away from Psyche's rolling surface in a curved path.

Cleared of Psyche's gravity well, remote-controlled guidance thrusters were engaged from Alpha-1 base and vectored the cargo's trajectory towards a 7-month glide path journey back towards Earth. If everything goes well at other drilling locations, there will be many more cargo cylinders launched to Earth in the future days from 16-Psyche.

Day-521

CHAPTER 31
PANTHIA CRATER'S REWARDS

The mining crew had packed up all of the surface equipment in preparation for moving to the next drilling site. Intense discussions had been exchanged between Alpha-1 and Alpha-3 crewmembers before *Panthia Crater* was democratically chosen as the next best site to drill for Psyche's rewards.

Panthia Crater had been chosen for several reasons. Properties obtained by satellite radar detected that inside the crater revealed excellent results. Panthia Crater had a highly reflective surface that speculated that it possibly contained extremely high rare metal elements. Specifically, it contained uranium, gold, silver, titanium, and some other unknown elements.

Alpha-3 simultaneously began unscrewing all five anchors and, in several minutes, floated free from its surface connection to Foxtrot Crater. Soft engine pulses ignited below the ship, and Alpha-3 rose steadily from a 4-mile depth inside Foxtrot Crater.

It hovered momentarily a hundred meters above the rim. Alpha-3 then vectored its direction southwest towards Panthia Crater. The ship proceeded slowly, and in five gentle flight minutes, the ship arrived above its new destination over top of Panthia Crater. Slowly it sank and touched down inside Panthia while bouncing slightly after the engines were shut down.

Day-522 thru Day-527 were hard work days used by the crew to laser install five anchor sleeves beneath Alpha-3 so that the ship could again be connected to the surface to allow downward pull in Panthia Crater.

Early 16-Psyche rise on Day-528, The Alpha-3 Miner began spinning its outer ring laser blades. As the blades touched the surface, sparks began angularly bouncing skyward as the hydraulics engaged its downward pull and began grinding into the hard reflective valuable metal surface.

Panthia Crater was loaded with precious rare metals. The laser blades had accomplished a depth of three inches in the first 24 hours, and the early results revealed that this was indeed the reason that they were here.

The early matter recovered was 59% pure gold, with 41% consisting of a dozen different rare isotopic metals. There were even some that were totally unknown to human science. It would take months of drilling to reach the two-meter limit of Alpha-3.

Results were so good that the process had completed filling one and a half more cargo pods by the end of the second month. Meanwhile, a second container pod of Psyche's rewards had been launched towards Earth for capture. The 16-Psyche mission was well on the way to being established and was now harvesting valuable rich metal resources from 16-Psyche.

Although a minority of the Alpha-2 mining digger ship had been lost along the way, the 40 surviving crewmembers had managed to salvage its nuclear reactor and many other valuable parts.

Alpha-1 had served well as a base for the 40 members that survived. Alpha-1 base was engineered to house all 50 had it been necessary. 10 Brave souls had been lost thus far in this mission. We honor their service as we proceed.

Panthia Crater had been so successful that it was decided to move the ship and drill again a half kilometer away. On Day-588, Alpha-3 began its move, and on Day-594, the ship was again set up, and the mining of rare minerals started up again inside Panthia Crater.

The mining process proceeded on schedule when Captain Jonathan Adams began planning an exploration mission to the bottom of Psyche's south pole to India, Eros, and Delta Crater. This was a mysterious area that the orbital satellite had not been able to examine from its gyrosyncronous position above the equator.

CHAPTER 32

INDIA, EROS, AND DELTA CRATER

On Day-611, Captain Jonathan Adams, Melissa Harper, and Austin Williams began their exploration sortie at 0900 hours. *India*, *Eros*, and *Delta Craters* are sites on Psyche that hadn't been explored.

From Alpha-1 base, the three springs launched a long flight southwest and glided above Psyche for 15 minutes. Their suit jets vectored them towards a touch down just past the inside edge of India Crater.

India Crater was rich with pure iron. India's dark black glassy floor was emitting ionized magnetic electrons sparks to the void of space. The magnetically charged sparkles being emitted would uniquely curve upward towards Psyche's North Pole. India Crater consisted mainly of pure iron, and its magnetic charge was causing Psyche to have a strong magnetic field of its own. The magnetic field was indeed helpful in protecting us astronauts from harmful solar radiation.

The three of us explored India Crater for an hour or so, then decided to take a short flight over to Eros Crater. There to our surprise, we discovered an ancient Ferro volcanism volcano that spewed molten iron a meter high in low gravity. Never would we have thought that a small molten oozing hot iron volcano could be present on this solar system object.

The volcano was ten meters tall with a meter diameter jagged peak nozzle that was slowly pushing toothpaste-like excretions of molten iron and curling around the mound as the iron quickly cooled and solidified as it touched each layer beneath.

Solidified molten iron layers cooled from the base to the top as they first fell and touched the lower ring, then gently began climbing while lapping upward, causing slopped circle ridges to form all over the top. Psyche indeed had an inner hot spot, and its source wasn't very far from the south pole and Delta Crater.

Delta Crater was located specifically at Psyche's South Pole rotation point. A two-minute flight now set the three astronauts down near the edge of Delta Crater.

CHAPTER 33
THE METALMITES

Our six eyes grew wide open at what we were now viewing through our space helmet shields. This 2-mile diameter crater was saturated inside with three-inch half-ball black bouncing objects. There were millions of them. From the crater floor, they simultaneously began vibrating, and all rose up a meter high and floated for a half minute. Then after two seconds of flight, they all gently settled to the surface. As they repeated this bouncing process, they again began vibrating every time they touched the floor of Delta Crater.

We looked at each other with astonishment, and Melissa spoke out first. "This magnetometer shows that the South Pole reverses its magnetic charge from positive to negative approximately every 30 seconds."

"Readings from my analyzer suggest that the bottoms of all of these black 3-inch half-ball creatures always retain a positive magnetic charge. When the positive charge of Psyche's pole is located at the South Pole for approximately thirty seconds, the metal creatures are repelled from the surface and will float." Melissa reported.

"Wait a minute," Austin injected. "We definitely need to examine several of those black magnet creatures. If I'm careful, I think I can safely retrieve some samples."

Austin engaged a slight spring thrust, and his suit rockets allowed him to hover over the crater's edge at arm's length. He used a magnetic stick tool to grab two of the black critters and placed them into a containment bag on his belt. He then turned and flew back towards

Melissa and Jonathan. Austin landed in the center between the two and opened the bag to expose the two samples.

Melissa's gloved hand carefully reached in to pick up one of the coal-black critters. "It's not vibrating now," she said. The metal critter then fell from her gloved fingers, settled to the surface, and began vibrating. Thirty seconds later, the critter floated a meter above the surface.

When the half-ball black creatures are touching the surface, each creature has many tiny bladed teeth for ingestion, and the tiny blades seem to be gnawing at the surface and eating dusty matter every time they land.

"This is totally amazing," Melissa continued. Austin and Jonathan agreed.

"Wow!" Melissa exclaimed.

"It got pulled from my hands when opposite poles were present, and now it floats above the surface again when like poles are presented."

Jonathan reached down, picked the fallen critter up, and turned it upside down to examine it more closely. "This thing has many tiny razor angled feet that must serve as mouths to ingest the dust matter it consumes."

"It's simply amazing that those things can actually survive in an airless vacuum," Austin chimed in. "There might even be a billion of these things. No one ever thought there would be any life forms here."

"It is yet to be discerned whether they are living or not. These things exist and are here in front of us. We should take these two samples back to the base and analyze them there."

"Sounds like a good plan," Austin said.

"We'd better head back to Alpha-1," Jonathan replied.

With the two critters stored away in Austin's backpack, they silently sailed away from Delta crater on a 20-minute flight that landed them back at Alpha-1 Base. Melissa had serendipitously named the sample critters *Metalmites*.

"Actually, we may even be able to engineer a larger version of a mining machine that will duplicate their actions and help the mining process of Psyche," Jonathan stated his postulation over the radio as they flew home.

Tragically, we made a mistake, overlooked protocols upon decontamination, and exposed the samples to air pressure. The Metalmites critters ceased to vibrate. A thorough laser examination in the lab revealed that the critters had a very condensed all-metal titanium shell with a tiny jelly-like brain muscle mass at their centers.

"We will ship a few dozen of these Metalmites back to Earth on the next cargo pod and let the scientist examine them in more detail. Who knows, these Metalmites might be worth a lot of money too." Jonathan queried

Their metal structure matter is so dense that one of these 3-inch Metalmites would weigh approximately 150 pounds on Earth. The metal they feed on in Delta Crater is super compressed and has probably been eating the metal floor for centuries. We'll definitely need further research from Earth at a later date. Live samples will be retrieved and kept under vacuum conditions when we ship the samples to Earth.

Many good days of mining continued, and we were now at the point of launching one cargo pod per month back towards Earth. Profit reports were excellent, but the fact that we had only one mining vessel certainly lowered our original intended output. However, this venture was turning into a very lucrative operation.

We had recently been made aware that Alpha-4 was being built in Mars orbit, and upon its completion on Day-883, it would be launched on a direct path to 16-Psyche that would take only 155 days. Since it was launched on a direct intercept course with Psyche, Alpha-4 is scheduled to arrive on Day-1087 of our mission. If all goes well with Alpha-4's journey, we should be double mining by Day-1095. That Day-1095 will mark our third year since our departure from Gateway Moon Base.

CHAPTER 34

REVAMPING ALPHA-3

The Alpha-3 mining digger so far had performed well, but necessary repairs had to be made to many of its overworked parts. Alpha-3 had to be shut down for two months to salvage the valuable diamond blades from Alpha-2's remains and then reinstalled on Alpha-3.

Shut down of Alpha-3 began on Day-962 and lasted until Day-1019. Teams of workers were dispatched on many work sorties to retrieve the blades and lasers from the derelict Alpha-2. It took many teams of astronauts almost 16-days to remove all of the salvageable blades from Alpha-2, and it took a month after that to uninstall Alpha-3's old blades and reinstall the new blades on Alpha-3. Many other parts had to be replaced on Alpha-3, and we were thankful that we could salvage 60% of Alpha 2's lasers. Over several months, work teams were able to accomplish revamping Alpha-3 to an excellent working mining digger machine.

By Day-1020, Alpha-3 was back in business and chewing up Psyche's recourses. Again cargo ships were being loaded to depart towards rendezvous with earth. For two more months, the Alpha-3 crew mined the rewards of Psyche while anticipating the arrival of Alpha-4.

On Day-1095, Alpha-4 arrived with a crew of 10 aboard. All went as planned as Alpha-4 soon landed gently near Alpha-1 base. By Day-1104, Alpha-4 was set up in the southern polar area near Delta Crater and began processing matter from Psyche. All went well for the next 500 Earth-days, with both mining ships producing a return load every 15 Earth-days.

CHAPTER 35
DEPART FOR HOME VIA CERES

On Day-1630, I, Jonathan Adams, and nine other crewmembers were scheduled to return home from our four-and-a-half-year mission. On Day-1629, I gladly turned my Head Commander duties over to Commander Frederick Crews, who had agreed to stay another year until the next ten members were scheduled to return home.

Early morning on Day-1630, nine crewmembers and myself departed 16-Psyche and headed towards home with a planned exploration stop at Ceres that humans had never explored.

It had been determined precisely that Ceres, the *Dwarf Planet*, was in perfect conjunction with Mars's orbital approach. Our return home shuttle called *Alpha-B*, would be in close proximity to Ceres on our journey home, and since humans had never explored Ceres, our return to Mars base would allow for a ten-day exploration of this mysterious world named Ceres.

Ceres is a round 946-kilometer or 588-mile diameter world that orbits the sun every 4.6 earth years on the inside of the asteroid belt. It is postulated by many scientists that it has an ocean of salty water below its icy frozen crust. Ceres rotates on its axis once every nine hours. Not much is known about this planetoid. The world has never been considered to possess any potential valuable rare minerals. Past astronomers had predicted that liquid water existed beneath the cold world's frozen crust.

Where there is water, there's always the possibility of life. As a final mission detail for this homeward-bound crew of ten explorers, it was our assigned duty detail to go where no humans had gone before and have the proper equipment to find the truth.

Our planned mission was to land and spend 10-days exploring this largest body in the asteroid belt. Ceres was the first asteroid ever discovered in the early days of astronomy.

On January 1st in the year 1801, Giuseppe Piazzi discovered Ceres at Palermo Astronomical Observatory in Sicily. Ceres is named for the Roman goddess of the harvester of corn. Ceres comes from the word cereal in modern language.

In 2015, a robotic satellite named *Dawn* visited Ceres and learned some interesting facts about its specifics, but at that point in time, humans had never set foot upon this icy low gravity planetoid. If all goes well on our return trajectory, this crew of 10 aboard Alpha-B will be the first humans to explore this frozen world tucked just inside the asteroid belt.

Alpha-B was a triangular-shaped shuttle about 50-meters in diameter. The ship was quite capable of easily landing on low-gravity Ceres, and this exploration mission's goal would be to ascertain how far the salty ocean exists below the icy crust.

Alpha-B was equipped with a sophisticated laser drill probe that could melt the crust and sink a visual probe through the ice to see if any life could possibly exist in the deep salty ocean below the icy crust.

CHAPTER 36

EXPLORING CERES

It had been 110 days since we left 16-Psyche, and we were approaching Ceres on Day-1740. I, Jonathan Adams, piloted the shuttle into an orbit of 100 kilometers above the surface of the Dwarf Planet Ceres. After several observation orbits, I made the decision to land in Occator Crater. That's where the salt deposits had been pushed to the surface and where the Dawn spacecraft first discovered the salty brine circles in the year 2015.

I made the assumption that the icy crust would be thinner in that location. The laser drill probe should be able to break through to the salty liquid water below the surface.

The camera heat sink probe has a depth range of 8 kilometers or almost 5 miles. If that crust is any thicker than that, our probe will not be able to break through to the potential ocean beneath the crust.

From an orbit of ten kilometers above Ceres, Alpha-B matched Ceres's rotation speed and vectored its direction towards Occator Crater. Ion nuclear propulsions pulsed reverse thrust to control the shuttle's slow approach.

At 50-meters, the ship's repulsion jets increased to once every five seconds until Alpha-B literally hung 3-meters above the surface for 60 seconds. Shuttle-B slowly sank until it touched the surface with a slight bounce and settled upon the surface of Ceres. Alpha-B crew had arrived on scheduled time to allow for this important 10 Earth-day exploration mission.

On Day-1761, Scot Warden, Melissa Harper, and I were suited up and ready to explore Occator Crater.

"Be careful," I stated.

Low gravity here will allow a person to jump as high as 17 meters or 56 feet. That's way more gravity than Psyche or Phobos but light enough to travel a half-kilometer or so in one jump. Before we began our venture outside, we studied and reviewed a report on the salty brine inside Occator Crater.

About the Brine in Occator Crater

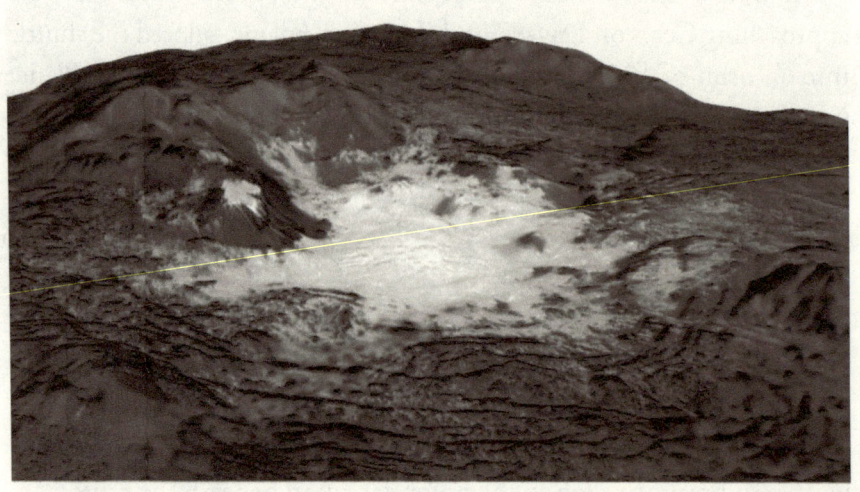

Ceres's Occator Crater

Before acquiring the highest-resolution data of Ceres, questions remained about the emplacement mechanism and source of Occator Crater's bright faculae or, in layman terms, the largest salt-brine bright spots discovered years ago by the Dawn spacecraft.

Occator Crater is about 92 kilometers or 57 miles in diameter. The brine effusion near the center of Occator Crater emplaced the faculae in a brine-limited impact-induced hydrothermal system that resulted from impact-derived fracturing from above and below that enabled brines to reach the surface and freeze.

The middle faculae named *Cerealia* and *Pasola Facula* postdated the central pit. They were primarily sourced from an impact-induced melt chamber, with some contribution from a deeper pre-existing brine reservoir.

In the crater floor, *Vinalia Faculae* were sourced from the laterally extensive deep reservoir only. Vinalia Faculae are comparatively thinner and display greater ballistic emplacement than the central faculae because the deep reservoir brines took a longer path to the surface and contained more gas than the shallower impact-induced melt chamber brines.

It was my decision to set the laser drill probe up in Vinalia Crater. The laser was in operation for an hour, and the laser drill probe began slowly melting into the icy crust. In another hour's time, the two-meter-tall probe had disappeared out of sight below the frozen surface.

It took another 24 hours, and at a depth of approximately 5 kilometers or 3.1 miles, the probe suddenly broke through to a liquid salty brine water ocean. With the probe now in liquid water, we returned inside the ship to activate the camera and sensors at the end of the probe.

On Phobos, an astronaut could jump 500-meters or approximately a quarter of a mile high. Gravity was also light, but not as light as the gravity on Phobos and Psyche. On Phobos, an astronaut could jump over half a mile high and possibly never come back down. So, an average person would be lucky if they could jump a half-meter high on Earth. Possibly, one could jump 3 meters or 10 feet high on Earth's Moon; here on Ceres, an astronaut could jump approximately 17 meters or 57 feet high.

After securing the drill site in several jumps, we returned to the safety of Alpha-B, which was positioned near the inside eastern edge of Occator Crater.

On Day-1764, the crewmembers gathered around the monitors. I, as Captain, gave the order to activate the deep-water camera on the tip of the heat-sink probe. Probe lights were activated and dark shadow-blue waters lit up a dull hazy video screen with the light barely penetrating a meter ahead in murky waters.

"The temperature of the waters is a warm 63 degrees Fahrenheit or 17 degrees Celsius", Melissa reported. "How could it be so warm below the frozen crust above?" Melissa asked.

"I don't know, but I'm guessing there must be some sort of inner heating going on deep below," Jonathan replied. "We still have approximately 3 kilometers of cable left. I suggest we send the probe into deeper waters to see the temperature and pressure below." Jonathan said.

CHAPTER 37
LIFE UNDER CERES FROZEN CRUST

Suddenly without warning, something struck the camera. A fast dark shadow flashed across the video, and the camera view was knocked around 50 degrees from a hovering mode orientation.

"Oh My!" Melissa shouted. "What in the world was that? We strained our focus upon the video monitor with a totally shocked expression."

"You must mean, what in this world is that?" Jonathan retorted. "I have no proper answer at the moment. Possibly the camera hit a rock or something," he suggested.

"No way!" Melissa replied. The probe was not moving in any direction when something knocked the underwater camera around. The camera still seems to be functional. Let's attempt to search the immediate vicinity. Melissa stated.

Melissa slowly rotated the camera counterclockwise until she reached 190 degrees and stopped with a yelping outburst.

"I SEE IT!" she exclaimed out loud.

The video blinked, then flashed into view on the shuttle forward cabin screen. Everyone was really shocked at what they were seeing on the monitor.

Jonathan turned and spoke to the nine other crewmembers.

"This is absolutely amazing," he said. "Those sea creatures are more than 10-meters in diameter and mostly round. That is except for the dent on its underside. It appears to me as some sort of opaque giant jellyfish-like creature that has a thousand or so teeth in its dented underbelly."

"The *creature* is emitting a high-frequency underwater sonic sound that is so high it's way above our frequency range to decipher," Melissa reported.

"Onboard computers are attempting to decipher the sound as we speak. The main computer is having difficulty doing so at the moment," Scot, the communication technician, reported. "I'm working on the problem," he replied to all.

The astonished crew watched as the 30-feet diameter creature slowly flexed its darker outer tips and moved in slow motion towards the searchlights of the camera probe.

Suddenly without warning, the creature's outer tip teeth began violently vibrating, and in another instant, the creature's underbelly was opening up and devouring the camera probe. A bright flash followed by static now appeared on all video monitors.

"Oh my!" Jonathan dreadfully replied. "If we were here fishing for knowledge, we've just found more knowledge than anyone ever dreamed. Life in this underwater Ceres Ocean is indeed a reality. There's no doubt anymore. I'm willing to bet there's abundant life on Jupiter and Saturn's moons as well," Jonathan stated.

"Yes indeed, that possibility just increased substantially," Melissa replied.

"More like a thousand percent," she stated.

Jonathan told Scot to retract the cable and install a new probe ASAP.

"Okay, but it's going to take 48 hours to retract and repair the cable and install a new camera probe," Scot replied. "I'll get on it right away, and I know that we have a little over five and a half days until we have to depart on our homeward journey."

"You're right," Jonathan replied. "Do your best to make it so, and we could get one more chance to investigate the below crust ocean before we leave for home."

"You've got it," Scot replied. "I'm on it immediately."

CHAPTER 38

SECOND CERES UNDERSEA PROBE

Early morning of Day-1767, crewmembers aboard Alpha-B gathered around the monitors to see what the second deep-water probe would reveal. The same sinkhole was used as before because deep down in the pre-drilled hole, the ice hadn't frozen back solid yet, making it easier for the second probe to submerge.

The screen lit up dark green at first as the searchlights attempted to peer through the undersea darkness.

"Visibility is about three meters with the new infrared camera installed. Thousands of floating plankton are in this salty water. We have two and a half kilometers or a mile and a half of cable left," Melissa reported.

"Okay, lets take it down deeper," Jonathan ordered.

At seven kilometers depth, there appeared floating undersea plant life the likes that had never been seen by human eyes before. Looking like something from a twentieth-century horror movie, red-leaved thorns squirted volatile poisons in several directions as the lights fell upon its thorns.

"Pull back quick!" Jonathan ordered. "It appears that the lights from the probe seem to threaten the plant. I think it is best not to antagonize it any further. It's all recorded, so let's move a little deeper past this undersea cliff edge.

"We can go one and a half more kilometer before we almost run out of cable," Scot informed.

"Right," Jonathan replied. "Take the probe down another kilometer, and let's see if any weird creatures exist under extreme water pressure conditions."

The probe cautiously proceeded downward past the cliff's edge into a dark ravine that reduced visibility to a meter in front of its projected floodlights.

"The probe has sunk within a half kilometer of the cable's limit," Scot reported.

"I suggest we pause the probe at this depth and save the existing 1,500 feet of cable in reserves," said Scot. Melissa sat at the probe's control and brought the probe to a stop, as suggested by Scot.

"It was indeed very dark and hardly anything could be made out in normal visual mode," Jonathan spoke up. "Switch the camera over to infrared mode and refine the downward radar to see if there is a solid surface below that is detectable."

The probe hovered slowly and began rotating clockwise as the infrared picture came up on the monitor view screen.

"OH MY!" was the crew's expression. In infrared, it's absolutely beautiful down there.

"It's beautiful all right," Scot chimed in. "But the water pressure down here is very extreme," he reported. "The water above exerts a pressure of 1,086 bars (15,750 psi), That's more than 1,071 times the standard atmospheric pressure at Earth's sea level. At this pressure, the density of water is increased by 5.95%. The temperature at the bottom is 1 to 4 °C (34 to 39 °F). Radar is detecting a bottom of molasses-like consistency that has properties of molten magnetic nickel-magnesium."

"That's amazing," Jonathan commented.

"Even the infrared was unable to detect a visual hard surface bottom to this trench. Radar could only reveal deeper shades of purple as it peered into the unknowable depth of Ceres's secrets. Switch the downward radar to horizontal, and let's see what's out there." Jonathan ordered.

The visual ahead showed up in red-tinted light and revealed for the first time that the probe was hanging halfway between two long tall underwater mountain ranges of ice. Millions of aquatic creatures were revealed to exist a half kilometer above the probe's lower location.

"Retract the probe up about 1,500 feet," Jonathan stated. "Evidently, the pressure down here is too much for any existing species above to handle. "

The probe had survived the extreme pressure so far, but the existing pressure along the cable was causing distortions in the video quality. As the probe approached the layer of life forms, a remarkable creature was revealed.

Ten times bigger than any Earth whale, a herd of five deep-blue dozen finned octagon-shaped crab-like creatures existed here. They, as a team, appeared to be floating on their backs and plucking morsels of star creatures sinking from the water level above.

There also existed schools of hairy rosy colored walrus-type creatures that darted upward like a missile for a half-kilometer, then gliding in an arc trajectory while then feasting upon smaller alien prey as they casually sank to the lower water level of their own pressure endurance before repeating the process all over again in five minutes time.

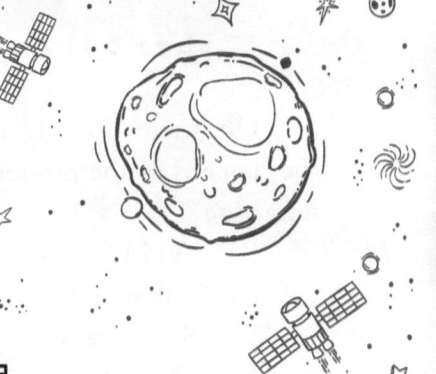

CHAPTER 39
SECOND CREATURE ATTACK

Melissa methodically panned the camera. Visibility was limited due to the darkness, but when the probe's lights suddenly fell upon an incredibly huge creature, it filled the entire monitor view screen. It suddenly flashed, filled the area with a two-second light pulse, and then began heading towards the probe.

"Quick," Jonathan ordered. "Cut the probe's lights."

"It's too late," Scot retorted. "The camera was no longer responding to any commands. It's gone." Scot said. "The computer's electronics are detecting that there is something on the end of the cable, but the electronics in the probe are totally fried. Whatever is down there, it must have swallowed the probe whole."

"I understand," Jonathan replied. "Attempt to retract the probe cable and playback the last of the recording just before the camera stopped."

"In work," Scot replied.

A freeze frame of a giant grotesque image filled the view screen as we all stood in awe of what we were seeing. Words were incapable of describing this thing. It resembled nothing ever recorded in earth's history. Its mass was so large that it would have been a thousand feet tall if it were placed upon the Earth's surface.

Thousands of hairy spider-like legs spun around in propeller-like motion and quickly propelled the creature in any direction it decided to go. It was attracted by the lights and decided to devour the probe.

"Oh, wait!" Scot vigorously injected, "I am attempting to retract the remains of the probe's cable, and suddenly the cable is resisting retraction."

"SAY WHAT?" Jonathan exclaimed. "You mean to tell me the creature swallowed the probe, and the cable is still attacked?"

"Yes," Scot answered. "In fact, whatever it is, it's pulling so hard that the motors cannot resist and the cable is now being pulled out again. There's less than a kilometer of cable left before it starts pulling on the ship," Scot advised.

"Okay then," Jonathan ordered. "Activate the laser and cut the probe's cable near where it enters the surface."

Scot immediately programmed the computer to vector the laser towards the surface cable that connected the probe to the ship.

In a bright arched fire, the laser began projecting its hot beam on an inch diameter titanium cable ten meters outside the ship's perimeter.

"It will take 94 more seconds before the laser is able to cut through that titanium cable," Scot reported.

Melissa spoke up. "There's only about 96-meters before the cable reaches the end. The creature is now pulling the cable backward at 3-meters per second. In 30-seconds, the cable will be taunt and start pulling the ship towards where the cable submerges below the surface."

"Give me 100% emergency power to the laser," Jonathan ordered.

All lights dimmed as the ship's full nuclear reactor focused its power on the laser rays upon the surface, attempting to fry the cable before the creature damaged the shuttle.

"There are only 11-meters left and about 4-seconds to cable impact," Melissa reported.

"Get ready for impact!" she yelled.

Alpha-B was jerked sideways from the creature's pull as the hot molten cable snapped and released its connection to the shuttle. The creature's strong pull force was able to complete the job before the laser finished cutting the cable.

The shuttle was jerked 2-meters sideways before settling again on the dusty surface. Besides a jerk from the cable snap, there appeared to be no immediate danger or significant damage to the ship. We were relieved that the cable had broken just in time, and the ship and crew were now safe again.

After a 30-second silent pause, Jonathan laughed slightly as he spoke. "It looks like we caught a bigger creature than we could handle. We're so lucky that the cable snapped just in time."

"We will analyze all the video data later," he stated. We have two days left before we are required to launch from Ceres on our homeward journey. We need to gather all the surface equipment and use the next two days to ensure everything is ready to depart Ceres.

"One thing is for certain," Jonathan stated. "There is definitely a second genesis of life below the frozen crust here on Ceres. It's always been postulated, but now it has been proven."

"We are definitely not alone. Life must also exist under Jupiter and Saturn's moons' icy surface. Further exploration here on Ceres will have to be left to future explorers. Our priority now is to get Alpha-B Shuttle ready to take us home."

We've all had a fantastic journey so far. I depend on the entire crew to ensure we are ready to leave this world.

"Let's get to work and get it done," Captain Jonathan ordered. We must launch on schedule, or the trip to Mars Base will take more time.

CHAPTER 40
THE JOURNEY HOME

It was Day-1770, and the overworked crew had diligently worked to ready Alpha-B for its launch on their four more month journey back to Mars Base.

Ceres had been a source of great discovery, and we now knew that life had developed elsewhere in our own solar system. There deep beneath the frozen crust of Ceres, exist many alien sea creatures. The loss of two cameras and the short video footage is enough to support our claims, and it will be submitted to scientists on Earth for better analysis.

Further study of Ceres would have to wait for the time being. Alpha-B and Crew were now in startup maneuvers in preparation for its launch towards Mars Base.

Launch day, Day-1772, at 0800 hours, Shuttle-B began retracting its screw-anchors attaching the craft to Ceres.

Shuttle-B increased its engine thrust to just above Ceres's light gravity bouncy point. The ship ascended slowly at first, then rose up three meters above the surface and hovered there for 30 seconds.

Climbing high in several minutes' time, Shuttle-B reached an altitude of two kilometers above Ceres. Nuclear-Ion engines ignited, and the ship arched over and fell ahead of Ceres's orbital path. As the ship swung around behind Ceres at a programmed point, the main engines throttled up and put the ship on an inward vector that was the precise trajectory required to rendezvous with Planet Mars's orbital position in approximately 115 days.

The vibration through the ship's hull stopped as the engines ceased propulsion. Shuttle-B had obtained its escape velocity, and the engines were now extinguished.

Shuttle-B and all aboard sailed silently at approximately six miles per second towards the far away Mars encounter that would take almost four more months to arrive. Shuttle-B would travel a total distance of over 60 million miles by the time it reaches Mars Base on Day-1886.

The crew watched intently as Ceres fell from the view of our homebound destination. King Jupiter in the far distance presented a spectacular grand view of our retreat from the millions of orbital bodies existing in the asteroid belt. We were on our way home. We considered Mars Base as home because it would supply all the resources required to take us to our real home planet Earth.

If all goes well, Alpha-B and crew will arrive at Mars in 114 days or Day-1886 since we first left Gateway Base just a little over five years ago. Or, to be more precise, that would equate to 5 years and 16 Earth-day rotations.

All ten crew members were required to spend at least two hours a day in the shuttle's spin gravity simulator for the next few months. This wheel-shaped 8-meter diameter gravity simulator could spin up to four astronauts at a time and expose them to forty percent earth gravity. The gravity simulator could also spin two astronauts up to a high rotation speed to simulate Earth's gravity.

I, Jonathan Adams, along with Melissa, would be exposing ourselves to earth spin simulation for two hours a day. As soon as my entire mission journal has been submitted to Mine-X Corp, Melissa and I will be boarding an Earth-bound shuttle that would require seven more months of travel time.

For over five years, our human bodies had existed on low gravity worlds, and our bone structure had to be built back up again before reaching Mars or Earth. Also, a strict bone enhancer diet was mandatory for all aboard. The bottom line was that all aboard were tasked with extra exercise periods to prepare for the upcoming Mars return.

Mars's gravity was only 38% of Earth's gravity, but even that amount of gravity was way more than they had experienced for nearly five years. We were all glad to be returning to the safety of Mars Base. The months passed without incident, and we were getting close and now only ten days away from Mars Base rendezvous.

On Day-1876 aboard Shuttle-B, the crew was extremely busy preparing the ship for Mars orbit insertion in ten-earth rotation periods.

Planet Mars was becoming somewhat prevalent in the forward monitor screen. Both moons appeared in the far distance as potato-shaped reflections, with Phobos barely visible moving swiftly behind Mars. All nine crewmembers and I were diligent at work in preparation for the upcoming insertion into Mars orbit.

CHAPTER 41

METEORITE DAMAGE

There wasn't any warning. Suddenly a loud explosion occurred under the shuttle directly below the main command deck. I, Captain Adams, only remember opening my blurred vision eyes and seeing and smelling noxious gasses escaping into the cabin. Two others and I were pinned against the wall in the total darkness of the shuttle's main command deck. Shuttle-B was spinning out of control. Barely conscious, I somehow managed to free myself against the pull of centrifugal gravity and climb back into the main command chair.

The pain in my head seemed intense, and the spin of the ship and extreme noxious gasses were causing me to convulse my stomach's content against the outside wall where Melissa and Scot were still unconscious.

I was extremely dazed and confused, but I somehow managed to take control of the serious situation. Under extreme stress, I strained against gravity to engage the main backup breaker.

The computer panel flashed to life, and the shuttle's side rockets fired to regain control of the spinning craft. Thirty seconds later, I sat there dazed and confused, watching two unconscious shipmates suspended weightless five meters overhead in the command cabin ceiling.

Tiny drops of blood floated slightly above my right eye as I pushed off toward Melissa and Scot's floating bodies. The backup computers had taken control of shutting down the escaping gasses, and oxygen began flowing from the air vents again and filled the cabin with breathable air.

Scot began waking up first while coughing and expelling the harmful gas he had inhaled. I quickly realized that he would be okay, and I floated towards Melissa, using her body mass to stop most of my forward motion. I guided us towards a medical kit from my control chair and opened up a pack of ammonia inhaler revivers. I cupped the mask to Melissa's mouth and nose, squeezed her abdomen from behind, and forced her to inhale the reviver mixture. Her eyes popped open, and she began gasping for breath and coughing simultaneously.

It took just a few more seconds before she regained her senses, but she managed to etch out strained words.

"What Happened?"

"I don't know yet. I just woke up myself," I replied.

Scot had somewhat regained his composure and began floating towards the shuttle's control chairs, followed by Melissa and myself. I strapped into the left side of the command chair as Melissa began strapping herself into the right-side chair. Scot strapped into a chair behind Melissa and me.

Still dazed, I asked for a status report on the crew and ship as I attempted to reboot the ship's main computer. The backup computer is only able to read the ship's pressure status. It shows a loss of atmosphere in the storage compartment directly beneath this main deck.

"I suggested that we should hurry and put on our spacesuits and keep our helmets close at hand in case we lose our atmosphere."

"That's a good idea," Melissa said as we all released our straps and floated towards the storage cabinet on a wall 5-meters away. I was the first to return to my control module and begin trying to ascertain what had happened.

Communications were down, and I had no idea if any of the other seven were alive. The backup computer has engaged and stabilized the ship's spin. A loss of air pressure in the storage compartment had extinguished a fire that was burning before the storage compartment's atmosphere was lost to the vacuum of space. Scot and Melissa had re-entered their consoles after suiting up with their helmets attached to their tool belts.

Scot put on his helmet and proceeded to check out the status of the others on the lower deck below. Melissa and I were also putting our helmets on and pressurizing our suits.

"I'll keep in touch over the helmet radio," Scot stated as he floated away towards a hatchway near the rear.

Melissa and I began working piously on trying to reboot the mainframe computer to enable an explanation of what had just happened. Between the two of us, we managed to start the reboot process, and in several minutes, the main computer screen began reappearing, and all major systems seemed to be mostly intact and nominal.

Melissa reported that the computer is reporting a 16-inch hull breach in the forward lower cargo bay.

"Just then," Scot radioed. "All seven are safe here in the rear cargo bay, and the forward compartment is sealed with a vacuum existing in there. Everyone managed to exit the forward cargo bay before the air supply was depleted. We're all okay down here, but an EVA will have to be performed to patch the damage to the cargo bay before we reach Mars." Scot finished his report.

"Acknowledged," I replied. "We're still on course, and what collided with the shuttle is unclear at the moment. Whatever it was, it couldn't have been too large, but it traveled at a tremendous speed rate upon impact. It's a good thing it only grazed the edge of the cargo storage pod. It could have been much worse." Jonathan said

"You ready the repair equipment, and I'll join you at the outer pressure chamber in five minutes." I radioed Scot. "You and I will perform the EVA to attempt to repair the hull damage."

"Roger that," Scot replied. "I'll meet you there shortly."

Leaving Melissa in charge, I floated swiftly through the ship to where Scot was waiting at the decompression chamber that would take us to the outside and the vacuum of space. Scot had already loaded the welder and materials we would need to repair the hull. We could barely squeeze into the chamber with our backpacks pressing against opposite walls. The door sealed, and in 30 seconds, all the air pressure had been released into space. The outer hatch opened and revealed thousands of visible stars surrounded by the double blackness of space.

I first squeezed and floated free out of the door while hooking my tether to the port outer hatch ring. I reached back inside the hatch and retrieved the welder. When it was floated out of the hatch, I attached a tether to the welder with the other end attached to my tool belt.

Scot soon exited, attaching his tether to the aft side of the outer hatch ring with two 24-inch square repair panels attached to his right suit leg.

"Go slow," I told Scot. "The corners of those panels could possibly damage your spacesuit."

"I hear you," Scot replied. "You go first, and I'll follow right behind you."

"Okay," I replied. "I'm headed under the forward cargo bay to see how big the rupture is."

At the end of my spoken words, another explosion occurred as I rounded the underside of the shuttle. My x-ray visor activated and protected my eyes from the brilliant flash 10-meters ahead of my position.

Scot followed shortly, not seeing the explosion that I had just viewed. I could only see the bright flash but couldn't see where it happened because, thankfully, I was behind the ship's edge.

"Connect your tether to the handrail beside me," I replied. "I surmise that there has been another explosion inside the damaged cargo bay. Possibly, an electrical spark has caused another oxygen canister to explode. It's a good thing that the bay was already depressurized, and there appears to be no fire inside. You watch my six while I release my tether and fly over the site with my space pack."

"Roger that," Scot replied.

As I approached the somewhat-round jagged 16-inch rupture, I could see that broken electrical wires were arching sparks against a metal ground source. I immediately contacted Melissa and had her shut down all electrical power to both cargo sections. The arching stopped, and I radioed Scot to come ahead with the repair panels.

"I think it's safe now to weld the panels over the rupture."

"Okay," Scot replied. "I'm almost there. "

Scot activated his magnetic boots and attached his feet just past the sixteen-inch jagged rupture. He stowed one panel to the side with a magnetic clip. I ignited the welding torch and began melting away the rough edges around the jagged hole. When I was through, Scot lowered the panel between the metal seams over the rupture.

I then attached my boots to the ship in front of Scot and began readying the welder while Scot attached temporary magnets to the panel's edge and backed away to allow me to tact weld two spots near the panel's edge.

Scot then moved back in to remove the temporary magnet clips. As he backed away again, I began completing the weld around the two-foot square perimeter of the panel. It was a slow process, and the first-panel weld took about an hour to complete.

Scot had been using his torch to smooth the edges of the second rupture approximately 3-meters away from the first repair. Just as I finished the first rupture weld, Scot was in the process of attaching the second plate over an oval-shaped 14-inch hole with the same two magnetic clips he had used before. I cautiously moved over to where the second plate was in place and quickly welded the two corners as Scot moved back in to remove the magnetic clips.

In five hours and 37-minutes of EVA time, Scot and I had managed to repair the damage to both holes in the cargo bay. We were in the process of packing up our equipment when it happened.

CHAPTER 42
GHOSTLY COMRADE ENCOUNTER

Scot and I stood attached to the hull with our helmets tilted back as far as our suits would allow. We saw something that was extraordinarily amazing.

Now descending upon the ship were ten ghostly white aberrations, each resembling a butterfly shape at first. Then the gaseous cloud split and morphed into the individual faces of the ten lost crewmembers.

"Am I dreaming?" I asked Scot.

"No way!" Scot replied. "I'm seeing this too."

"We're seeing this also," Melissa reported from inside.

"How can this be?" She questioned. "Their lips are moving, but no sound is discernible."

Melissa programmed their simultaneous lip movements into the computer's memory banks in an attempt to translate their words. In several calculated translation minutes, the computer replied to the task assigned.

The aberrations are speaking in simultaneous harmony, the computer replied. It appears that their synchronized lip movements mimicked the exact three simple English words. The computer translates the lip-sink to the words "*We are Home.*" The ten ghostly figures then gently evaporated into their new realm of existence when their message was deciphered.

FINAL-CONCLUSION-REPORT

Day-1884, Shuttle-B was two days away from Mars orbit insertion. We were so close now that we considered ourselves safely home.

I, Captain Jonathan Adams, used these last two days to compile all my recorded data and experiences of my lead role in setting up the mining operation of the 16-Psyche mission. This entire chaptered report will be issued to Mine-X Corporation on Day-1886 of this mission.

February 3rd, 2243

To Griffin Exa Musk and the 30- members of the CEO Mine-X Corporation in Houston Texas.

I, Jonathan Adams, do hereby submit this entire 16-Psyche legend of memoirs and experiences of all words included above. These chaptered words are my best recollections of my personal experiences of my lead role in being the first Commander involved in setting up the new 16-Psyche mining operation.

As of this filing date of February 3rd, 2243, it will have been five years and seventeen days since this mission first departed from Gateway Base. I consider this report the tender of my job that is now concluded as we enter Mars insertion. There were 10 of our best lost along the new journey's way. We are all home now. Captain Candice Roselle and the crew's dedication will forever be memorialized as heroes. They gave their all.

I personally considered myself extremely fortunate to have survived this unique mining adventure into the Asteroid Belt. In the most profound sorrow of all involved, the mission has lost ten of our bravest astronaut-miners along the way. Their souls are home also.

This first 16-Psyche crew has begun the most valuable mining adventure ever in this solar system. With much hard work, many more unique future treasures will be mined in future days.

Psyche-16 mining rewards have been all and more than anyone had ever dreamed. The valuable resources there will be continuously mined for decades to come.

My personal monetary rewards are substantial.

Besides my five-year pay of one hundred million-earth dollars per year for time served, I will receive a yearly severance pay of two billion dollars for the rest of my life. Psyche has and will produce many more wealthy individuals such as myself, a very lucrative future should they choose to serve.

Each crewmember, upon their return, will receive substantial pay also as per each of their individual agreement with Mine-X Mining Corp. (MXC)

I now have a seven-month journey to Planet Earth, but that seemed to be the easy part after all I have endured over the past five years.

To survive such a hazardous mission is a reward in itself. It's like knowing without a doubt, that you have earned every dollar of your pay.

That's a meaning that has ease of remaining life written upon the entire afterward experience. For five years, I was an explorer. I still am.

I'm nearly home now. Over the next seven months, I have time to contemplate my future. I truly know that the next reward is something more valuable than money could ever buy. That reward can only be duplicated by the experiences of the next daring mission ahead.

My present future thoughts lean toward a lush tropical home on the beautiful Planet Earth for at least the next five years. I'm only 27 now and not ready to retire. I simply need some contemplating rest on earth. The Good Earth! It's the best planet for humans in this solar system.

Mine-X Corporation (MXC) is now the wealthiest mining company in the solar system. They are the first true space heroes to go where no humans have before.

I, Jonathan Adams, am honored and grateful to have served in your employ. Hereby, on this mission Day-1886 from Mars orbit, I submit this report as my final commitment to Mine-X Corporation.

I, Captain Jonathan Adams, do hereby sign and submit my final report of my involvement in the 16-Psyche mission to all the officials of Mine-X Corporation (MXC).

Head Commander of the first 16-Psyche Mission.

Signed this date of February 3rd, 2243

Captain Jonathan Adams

1609 Pleasant View Drive.

Houston Texas 77007

Kind Regards!

ABOUT THE AUTHOR

Full Name,
Donald Eric Wilkins.

But!
I have always gone by Eric Wilkins
my entire life, and I always will.

Born, 1157 pm
December 24, 1950
Henderson N. C.

Loved Astronomy from an early age.

Lived many years on this
Fantastic Spaceship, *Earth*.

My Bucket List is almost complete,
and I will soon go on to
explore the Universe.

The Earth is moving toward Leo at a
dizzying speed of 390 kilometers a second.
That's a little over 242 miles per second.

You're on it too. God speed!

www.ingramcontent.com/pod-product-compliance
Lightning Source LLC
Chambersburg PA
CBHW020915180626
46816CB00007BA/2409